Otto P. Nudd

Also by Emily Butler

Freya & Zoose

Crown Books
for Young Readers
New York

Otto P. Nudd

Emily Butler

*illustrations
by Melissa Manwill*

All rights reserved. Published in the United States by Crown Books for Young Readers, an imprint of Random House Children's Books, a division of Penguin Random House LLC, New York.

Crown and the colophon are registered trademarks
of Penguin Random House LLC.

Visit us on the Web! rhcbooks.com

Educators and librarians, for a variety of teaching tools,
visit us at RHTeachersLibrarians.com

Library of Congress Cataloging-in-Publication Data is available upon request.
ISBN 978-1-5247-1775-9 (hardcover) — ISBN 978-1-5247-1776-6 (lib. bdg.) —
ISBN 978-1-5247-1777-3 (ebook)

The text of this book is set in 12-point Century Schoolbook Pro.
Interior design by Ken Crossland

Printed in the United States of America
10 9 8 7 6 5 4 3 2 1
First Edition

To David J. Butler,

man for the ages.

You did *not* inspire Otto.

You inspire me.

Contents

Otto P. Nudd

A Man, a Raven, and a Thingamajig

"Otto, you're splendid," mumbled Bartleby Doyle. "You're a genius. A bird for the ages."

His mouth was full of pins and it was hard to make out every word, but Otto had a good idea of what he was saying. If a raven could blush, Otto would have blushed. But not because he disagreed with Bartleby. Oh, no. The Old Man was right.

"The likelihood of this thingamajig going up in

flames is small," continued Bartleby. "But why take a chance if you don't have to?"

Otto winced. He disliked the word "thingamajig," preferring "machine," or even "contraption." But he was fussier than the Old Man, who was (for the greatest inventor Ida Valley had ever known) a casual, absentminded sort of human.

Bartleby bent over the length of moss-colored corduroy and pinned a strip of white fabric to it. The fabric was fireproof. It was, in fact, cut from the underwear of Ida Valley's fire chief. Bartleby never asked how Otto had obtained this item, but you should know that (1) it was scrupulously clean, and (2) the fire chief never left a basket of laundry unattended on the roof of his car again. At any rate, when Otto had pressed a flaming match to the garment and it had refused to ignite, Bartleby bought an entire case of underwear. Then they'd cut it all into the strips that now lay on the workbench.

Bartleby held out his hand. Otto gave him a strip, and then another, and another. Eventually, the corduroy was covered with overlapping white strips. Bartleby carried everything to a sewing machine under a long, high window through which the gray light of dawn shone, and sat down.

While the Old Man fiddled with the stitch length regulator, Otto looked about their workshop with immense satisfaction. They had all the good stuff. There were table saws of many kinds, and a drill press, and chests full of wrenches and screwdrivers. There were buckets of bolts, jars of nails, and a vast array of pulleys and gears. There were also many finer instruments, like strain gauges, flowmeters, and gadgets to measure acceleration and isolate vibrations. A water fountain dominated an entire corner of the shop, used by man and raven alike whenever they got thirsty. Otto loved that thing!

What couldn't a person (or bird) invent here?

Two details seemed out of place in the workshop. An empty birdcage protruded from behind some filing cabinets, and large burlap sacks bulging with peanuts were lined up against a wall, slumping over a little, as if they were taking a nap. Neither were items of curiosity to Otto. He had lived in the cage, and knew the nuts were part of a monthly delivery that had been going on since before he'd hatched.

The fact was that Bartleby was a peanut fanatic. He fed them to corvids, as we shall see, and he popped them into his own mouth like candy.

"Ready, my boy?" asked Bartleby.

Otto positioned himself on the other side of the sewing machine and gave Bartleby the smallest of nods. Without another word, the Old Man rammed his foot down on the floor pedal.

The machine jolted to life. Its needle gobbled through the fabric like a noisy demon, suturing the layers of cloth together faster and faster. Bartleby barely kept up with it, guiding the material over the feed dogs and back to Otto. The raven deftly plucked the pins out of the fabric as they passed him, thrusting each one into a round pincushion. He didn't miss any.

They made an excellent team.

When they were done, Bartleby shook the corduroy out and examined it for gaps between the seams. There were none. Otto checked it a second time, going over every stitch with eyes as keen as blades. Their work was good. It was more than good—it was super. Otto flew to Bartleby's shoulder and balanced there, imperious and bright. "Hello!" he cawed. "Hello!"

Deep, happy wrinkles puckered Bartleby's face. He stroked the exuberant ruff of feathers under Otto's throat as he walked to the door of their workshop. They would meet again after breakfast.

"We're ready, old bean," he said (even though Otto was a young bean). "Very, very ready. I can feel it in my bones. Today's the day."

2

The Inside Scoop

Pippa Sinclair stomped into the kitchen. She looked absolutely ferocious.

"Where's my yellow scoop? I can't find it anywhere. And I've turned the house inside out!"

"Turned the house inside out?" Mrs. Sinclair looked up from her list, the first of many she would scribble that day. "You just rolled out of bed."

"Where's my yellow scoop?" Pippa would not be sidetracked.

"I borrowed it a tiny bit," admitted Mrs. Sinclair. She knew she was guilty. "Just to plant the pansies. It's in the bag of garden soil."

Pippa stared at her mother in disbelief. "You mean the *dirt*?" she asked. "Mom, that scoop is strictly off-limits."

Mrs. Sinclair stared back at Pippa, their eyes locked in a contest of wills. Then Mrs. Sinclair surrendered. Pippa was formidable even when she was wrong. When she was right, she towered with moral authority.

"Off-limits!" repeated Pippa. "It's for the birds, and the birds only."

"It's for the birds," Mrs. Sinclair conceded, waving her list in defeat.

Pippa threw open the doors to the porch overlooking the backyard. There, by a clump of purple pansies, was the bag of garden soil. And sure enough, a yellow plastic handle emerged from its loamy surface.

"Not cool, Mom," said Pippa.

She sped outside, yanked the scoop out of the soil, and rapped it against the porch a little harder than was necessary. Then she unscrewed the lid on the five-gallon bucket of premium birdseed that she kept in the shade of a lilac bush. It was the delicious kind, with extra sunflower kernels. Pippa plunged the scoop into its depths several times, filling a mason jar with the blend of nuts, seeds, and dried berries. Then she carried the jar across the yard and set it at the base of the bird feeder.

Now came the hard part. The bird feeder hung six feet in the air, and Pippa was shrimpy, even for a ten-year-old. She used a long branch that forked at the tip to lift the feeder off its pole. After lowering it to the ground, she filled its hopper with birdseed from her jar. Then she hoisted it all the way back up. Her arms shook with effort.

"Come and get it!" she yelled.

She didn't wait to see who was going to show up first. She was running behind schedule, and there was still the question of Otto's gift.

Was anyone watching? She didn't think so.

Pippa sidled over to the Japanese maple whose long branches brushed the dirt like gentle brooms.

It offered good cover. She ducked under the leaves and put out a hand, touching the place where two roots met to form a little bowl. Yes, something was there—a hard, smooth, narrow thing, which Pippa slipped into the pocket of her jeans.

From her other pocket, she pulled out half a hamburger she'd saved from yesterday's dinner. It was squashed from spending the night in her sock drawer. *Otto won't care,* she thought. *He's not picky.* She put it in the spot between the roots and backed away, emerging from the tree and wiping her palms on her shirt.

"Hello, Otto! Hello!" she shouted into the woods behind her house.

Now Pippa was just plain late. Mr. Doyle, her next-door neighbor, was probably waiting for her.

"Eat something. Eat a muffin, at least," nagged Mrs. Sinclair as Pippa whizzed back through the kitchen.

There was no time to eat a muffin. She'd chew a handful of birdseed on the way to school. Some days were like that. But she couldn't leave the house without checking her treasures.

Pippa ran up to her bedroom and pulled a fishing

tackle box from under her bed. She flipped the lid open, and there they were, the things Otto had left for her under the tree. Each treasure was in its own compartment. There was a large assortment of buttons, both brass and plastic. There was a bracelet with a broken clasp, and a silver charm shaped like a sailboat. There was a new tube of ChapStick and several bottle caps. Paper clips and polished rocks and a lens from a pair of sunglasses. Clamshells and a green foam dart and three dimes. Nuts and bolts fused together with orange rust. An earring.

Pippa reached into her pocket and pulled out this morning's gift.

"Oh," she breathed. "Oh, Otto. It's sublime."

She stroked the flawless curve of a white porcelain handle with her fingertip. It still had some of the teacup attached. It *was* sublime.

3

Folks Oughta Mind Their Own Business

Otto P. Nudd was raised in captivity, but by dint of hard work and shrewdness, he was now a free bird. "A true raven will not be shackled" was his personal slogan, and he repeated it now as he tiptoed into his own home.

"You mean the way I'm shackled to this thing?" asked Lucille from the far side of the living room.

Otto jumped. He hadn't realized she was awake

and rocking the incubator like a crib. Was she teasing him? Otto thought so but wasn't a hundred percent sure. They were practically newlyweds, and he was still getting used to her playfulness.

Lucille gave him a reassuring roll of her black eyes, and he relaxed.

"How'd you sleep, dear?" she inquired. "You left before the sun was up."

"I slept well, thank you," he said.

Otto was an early bird by nature. What Lucille didn't know was how many predawn hours her husband spent with the Old Man, himself an early riser. Frankly, she didn't know because Otto didn't tell her. He wasn't sure she'd appreciate how much time he spent in the workshop inventing things, now that they were expecting their first chick.

Of course, Lucille understood that Otto was an inventor. *That* was no secret. Theirs was an uncommonly fine nest—Lucille knew just how fine it was, because she had built it herself—but Otto was the one who had filled it with all sorts of devices of his own making. He was an inventor of many things, and she loved that about him.

Now he sat on the couch and flipped through the

issue of *Popular Science* he'd fished out of a dumpster behind the ShopRite. Why humans threw away such prizes he'd never know! He particularly liked the article about motor oil filtration, and had read it many times.

"'Sludge will destroy an engine,'" he murmured to himself, turning the page.

"Down with sludge!" agreed Lucille.

She stepped lightly on a spring-loaded trapdoor in the floor of their nest, and it popped open with a *whoosh*. A hole was revealed, and through it, she kicked some shriveled grapes and an onion ring, remnants of last night's meal. Lucille did not care for leftovers. She closed the door and covered it with a straw mat.

"What are your plans for the day, my love?" she asked.

"Oh, just the usual. Making sure the neighborhood isn't going to heck in a handbasket—that sort of thing." Otto did not mention the Great Experiment that was to take place behind the workshop later that morning. He should have, but he didn't. "What are *your* plans for the day?"

"Hmmm," she said slowly, as if giving the question

her full consideration. "The first thing I'm going to do is find a bird who knows a thing or two about fixing incubators."

When this failed to elicit a response, she persevered. "Because our incubator is on the fritz. The fritz! At this rate, I'm going to have to sit on our egg myself."

Otto was engrossed in an advertisement for double-handle wrenches.

"Maybe I'll take a crack at it," said Lucille. "I know a thing or two about vices."

"Devices. *De-vices.* Never call them 'vices,' for that is what they are not." Otto sighed and closed the magazine. "Now, what are you going to crack?"

"The incubator, dear. Our egg is cooling down."

Seventeen days ago, Lucille had carefully deposited an egg into the incubator, designed and built by Otto. Other birds sat on their eggs, never leaving an unhatched brood for longer than a few minutes. Lucille was far too modern to adopt that practice. Still, she turned the egg every quarter hour, and it was getting cold. No ifs, ands, or buts about it.

"Impossible," said Otto.

He crossed the nest to examine the large box built out of plywood scavenged from the town dump. It sat on four sturdy legs and featured a viewing window. With a simple twist of a crank, an adjustable shelf within the box tilted back and forth, allowing the egg to be turned. (An unturned egg, it was felt, would result in an addlebrained chick, and Otto was having none of that.) The most remarkable part of the contraption was its side-mounted boiler, filled with water and heated by a small kerosene lamp. Once heated, the water was piped around the inside of the box, keeping the egg nice and toasty.

An open flame was, ordinarily, the last thing a raven would allow inside her nest. Indoor heating was an abomination to all birds, despised by even the most stupid. Only after Otto demonstrated the flameproof properties of the box a hundred times (it was lined with the same stuff he'd introduced to the Old Man) would Lucille consent to having it in her home. And now she could not do without it.

Otto saw the problem at once. He lifted the top off the box and adjusted the pipes. "All better now," he said to the egg, giving it a gentle nudge with his head in what he hoped was a paternal manner. Was this what a father would do? He guessed it might be, but he wasn't sure.

How did one act "fatherly," anyway? It wasn't as if the egg had come with an owner's manual, and *Popular Science* was strangely silent on the issue. Life would be different when the egg hatched, and the thought unnerved him. He might not do everything right. He might not do *anything* right. Well, the chick would show itself soon enough, and then he'd figure things out in the privacy of his own nest.

Or would he? To Otto's annoyance, their brood of one was enormously interesting to the neighborhood. It was practically turning into a community event.

"Folks oughta mind their own business," he told the egg.

"Why? It's an egg like no other!" cried Lucille stoutly.

"We should charge admission," Otto grumbled.

The egg was a full 50 percent larger than average. It was undeniably a raven egg, oblong and a mottled blue. But it was huge. Otto had never seen anything like it. Neither had their neighbors, who took every opportunity to cram themselves into the nest and goggle at the thing. It was a miracle, they said! It was a sign of the times!

"Do we pester our neighbors every time they hatch a batch?" asked Otto.

This made Lucille snort with laughter. "Hatch a batch! Who even says that anymore?"

"I do. Birds are too curious these days. They stick their beaks where they don't belong. They snoop," insisted Otto.

"You're so old-fashioned," Lucille said.

"I'm just a bird who likes his space," replied Otto.

"And I like you," said Lucille. She stepped on one of his feet with real affection, and held it tightly. "Thank you for fixing the incubator. I was worried about Ambrose. Or Bettina, if it's a girl."

She's named it, thought Otto with some pleasure. Still, he couldn't get over the magnitude of the thing. It struck him as unnatural. Preposterous. What if something was wrong? Maybe they should cover it with a blanket, just to keep the neighbors from speculating. . . .

"Lu-Lu-Lucille!" The black head and brawny shoulders of a mostly grown raven pushed through the window.

"Feathers!" swore Otto under his breath.

"Christopher, darling," sang Lucille.

Christopher was her little brother, and the apple of her eye. Otto found him annoying. With no siblings of his own (or at least none that he could remember), Otto failed to understand how Lucille could care so much about someone who wasn't . . . Otto.

"Good morning! How's Potato doing today? Everything okay in there?" asked Christopher. He regarded the egg with the tender benevolence of an uncle-to-be.

"Everything is lovely," cooed Lucille.

She turned the crank, and they watched as the egg rolled gently to the other side of the incubator. For a minute, nobody said anything. Then Christopher remembered the reason he'd come by.

"Otto!" he cawed, his voice breaking a little. "Old Man Bartleby just left the house. Thought you might like to know." He winked at Lucille.

That was that. Otto's day had officially begun. When Bartleby left the house, Otto left the house. Otto arranged his copy of *Popular Science* on the coffee table and gave Lucille a peck on the cheek.

"I'll be home for lunch," he said.

"Better pick something up," said Lucille.

"Righty-ho, wife," said Otto.

He flew smartly out the front door. It would not do to be late, and Otto P. Nudd never was.

4

Outraged by Marla's Theft

Pippa and Otto lived in Ida Valley, a place that smelled mostly of wheat bran and applesauce. This was hardly surprising, since the town manufactured 83 percent of all apple bran muffins sold in America. It manufactured every sort of muffin, in fact. There were days when Ida Valley smelled of blueberries and buttermilk. Occasionally, it reeked of mashed zucchini. When double chocolate-chunk muffins rolled off the line, people would take long walks and just breathe.

The houses lining Pippa's street had porches that wrapped all the way around them like old, comfortable aprons. Each house had a deep backyard enclosed by a wooden fence in some stage of decay. It rained in Ida Valley—it rained a lot. The smell of rain, rotting wood, and muffins was simply intoxicating, once you got used to it.

Behind Pippa's fence was a small forest that included firs, cedars, and hemlocks. Otto lived in a tall Douglas fir from which he could see the roof of Pippa's house, and also the roof of her neighbor Bartleby Doyle. Otto shared his forest with owls, little brown bats, and banana slugs the size and shape of actual bananas. The place had its share of raccoons, fiendish agents of destruction that will become important to this story (as will a certain squirrel). If this weren't enough, a river ran through the forest, bringing with it a host of fish, great blue herons, and otters.

Taken all together, Ida Valley was a tremendous place for a girl and a raven to grow up.

Otto swooped down from his nest and landed on

the power line that ran from Pippa's house to Bartleby Doyle's and on down their street. From there, he watched Pippa burst out her front door and hurry to the sidewalk, where Bartleby stood waiting for her.

Pippa did not, as she had in years past, put her hand in Bartleby Doyle's. She was far too old for that now. A fifth grader could walk herself to school. She did not require an escort, thank you very much. But they liked their routine, and if something wasn't broken, why fix it? Besides, they had a lot to talk about.

"You won't believe what Otto gave me," Pippa began.

"Tell me everything," said Bartleby.

"Well," said Pippa, "you know how he's been leaving lots of buttons lately?"

"Buttons galore!" said Bartleby.

"This morning, I went to the place"—Bartleby Doyle knew all about the place—"and he left me a teacup. Or the best part of the teacup. Wouldn't you say the handle is the best part? I would. Definitely."

And then they were off, walking the seven blocks to Pippa's school while exchanging views on their favorite subject: corvids.

Corvids, you ask? Yes, corvids! They were absolutely obsessed with corvids. This came as no surprise to Otto. Corvids were the smartest animals on the planet. Everyone knew that. Magpies, crows, rooks, jackdaws, blue jays—corvids, all. And ravens were corvid royalty. The cream of the crop. Top bird.

You've seen the best, so forget the rest, thought Otto, ruffling his glossy neck feathers with pride.

He flew from utility pole to utility pole, always keeping an eye on his friends. If they ever needed his help, he'd be there. Plus, there were snacks at stake.

A long green park lay between Pippa's house and her elementary school. She and Bartleby could have shaved fifteen minutes off their commute by taking the path that cut across the grass. This they did not do. Instead, they strolled along the charming split-rail fence that bordered the park. Some days, they went left, and other days right. But walking around the park had been their routine for years.

On this morning, as on all the others, Bartleby produced a paper bag from his pocket and handed it to Pippa. Pippa opened the bag and removed one peanut (unsalted!). She placed it on the first post of the fence. Then they continued down the line, stopping every eleven feet to deposit another peanut. At the corner of the park, they turned right and kept going until every post along their route was festooned with a delectable treat.

Otto watched them fondly. He knew the peanuts were meant for the neighborhood corvids. As top bird, he was entitled to his choice of peanuts, which he snatched up as soon as the school bell rang. Then, and only then, would the local crows, magpies, and jays flock to the fence and help themselves. This was the natural order of things. Everyone respected the natural order.

That is, almost everyone.

Out of the corner of his eye, Otto saw a bundle of gray fur shoot out from behind a bush, dash up a fence post, and dash back down. Where a peanut had been just seconds earlier, now there was nothing.

Otto shook his head, blinking hard. *What was that?* he asked himself.

Then it happened again. A blur of motion streaked along the top of a rail so fast that Otto could hardly believe it. But who could argue with an empty post? Somebody was stealing the snacks!

By the time the third peanut disappeared, Otto

moved in for a closer look. From his perch on the branch of a nearby pine, he watched as a fourth peanut practically vanished. Now he was able to identify the culprit. It was Marla, a neighborhood nuisance, a squirrel of ill repute.

"Thief!" hissed Otto.

This didn't slow Marla down one bit. She stuffed a fifth peanut into her swollen cheek and raced toward the next post.

"You there!" Otto called. "Back away from that peanut!"

Marla grabbed peanut number six.

"Stop immediately! Cease and desist!" cawed Otto. His eyes bulged with outrage.

Marla did not stop. A seventh peanut was poached.

"Quit it!" Otto shrieked.

He launched himself from his branch and flew straight at the squirrel. He'd swat that peanut right out of her paw, so help him.

But Marla was too fast. She popped the peanut into her cheek, raced down the post, and was almost out of sight before Otto even landed on the rail. Her final act was to turn and make an extraordinarily rude gesture in Otto's direction. Then she was gone.

5

Bartleby Brains Himself

Otto sat on the rail for a few moments, trying to understand what had just happened. Marla, a mere squirrel, a nobody, had stolen seven peanuts. Seven! A single peanut would have been too many. Peanuts weren't meant for squirrels. They were for Otto (first and foremost) and then for other birds. Nobody questioned this arrangement. It was beyond dispute.

Something would have to be done about Marla.

Now the sun was well above the treetops. *Time stands still for no raven,* thought Otto. He strode along the fence with dignity, his head held high. He hoped no one had witnessed Marla's defiance. Disrespect eroded the social order. Otto gulped down the first peanut he came to. It tasted rancid. Little by little, he got a grip on himself. He had things to do before the Great Experiment, and not much time in which to do them. Duty called.

Otto spread his wings for liftoff, determined to put all thoughts of Marla out of his mind until later.

His tasks began with a thorough inspection of the neighborhood's gutters. He paid special attention to the storm drains. These could become clogged with garbage, and when that happened, the streets would flood—good for the frogs and ducks, but bad for everyone else. Otto removed socks, deflated soccer balls, and clumps of leaves from the grates that covered the drains. Once, he even dislodged a filthy diaper.

Next, he inspected the power lines that ran along the streets. Children hardly older than Pippa had been observed tossing their sneakers over the wires, leaving them to dangle like earrings. Why did they do it? Why? Otto could not fathom the impulse that led humans to do a thing so idiotic. Up he would fly to the power line, deftly untying the sneakers and watching soberly as they dropped to the ground. Time permitting, he would unstring the laces and deposit each shoe in a garbage can on opposite sides of the neighborhood. That was a real strike for decency!

Today, the gutters and power lines were clear. Normally, this would fill Otto with a lofty sense of accomplishment. While species of smaller intellect spread disorder and confusion, Otto P. Nudd left the world in better shape than he found it. That's what made him top bird, all modesty aside. That's why he was king.

Not this morning, though. Otto took no pleasure in his work. Zero. His blood was still boiling. His head hurt. He could not stop thinking about Marla and the stolen peanuts. *Pull yourself together,* Otto thought. *The Old Man's back by now. It's time.*

He flew to the workshop, where he'd been raised and educated, where he'd worked as an apprentice of sorts, and where he returned almost every day.

He settled on the sill of the high window under the eaves. The thing with Marla had put him behind schedule, but he was confident that Bartleby was waiting for him. Otto peered in through the glass and was relieved to see the Old Man munching on some peanuts. That man loved peanuts as much as ravens did! Why, he had two unshelled peanuts stuffed in his ears, to block out noise!

Actually, this last part concerned Otto, who watched his friend amble around the workshop. How would he hear Otto tapping at the window? Tapping was their signal. Three taps let Bartleby know that Otto was ready to come in and get to work.

Otto tapped the window three times with his beak. Bartleby did not look up. Nervous, Otto tapped three more times. There was no sign Bartleby heard him. Otto hammered away, three times, six times, twelve times, a hundred times. He got no response at all.

The windows were made of very thick glass—that much Otto knew. His beak would break before the glass did. He stopped tapping.

This was quite a pickle.

Meanwhile, Bartleby Doyle moved about his workshop, cheerfully oblivious to the frantic tapping above his head. His mind was 99 percent focused on one thing: the Great Experiment that was about to take place. The remaining 1 percent wondered why on earth Otto was so late.

"Where is that bird?" Bartleby asked. "To be tardy today of all days!"

You might be asking why he didn't just look up. *Look up! Look up, Old Man!* you might be pleading, silently or otherwise.

But in Bartleby Doyle's defense, he'd been waiting for Otto for ages. He'd watched for his partner's familiar shape at the window and listened for his taps. Now it was getting late, and Bartleby was antsy.

He was also seventy-eight years old, and could be forgiven for not wanting to waste time. Arguably, he didn't have much of it left.

Bartleby lifted his hands to his ears and readjusted the peanuts, tuning them like the dials on an old radio. He turned them carefully, a little to the right, and then a little to the left. They were not, as he supposed, his hearing aids. Earlier that day, he had reached for the small acoustic devices on his dresser. Unfortunately, he had grabbed peanuts instead. An easy mistake—anyone could have made it!

But (mistake or no mistake) the result was this: Bartleby Doyle heard diddly-squat.

He hummed to himself with growing excitement. There was a skip in his step as he walked to a locker under the very window Otto was now beating with his wings. Bartleby opened the locker and admired the flying machine that hung from a hook. He clicked his heels together, almost giddy with anticipation.

"This is it, old bean!" he said (and he really was an old bean). "Time to take the plunge! Probably the wrong expression."

He giggled at his ridiculous choice of words.

Then he unzipped his baggy overalls, covered with the dust and debris of a thousand experiments, and let them fall to the floor. He stood for a moment in his ancient underpants, wrestling with a pang of remorse. Where was Otto? He was going to miss the triumph of their first flight together! Bartleby looked at his wristwatch and shrugged. There would be other flights. Lots of them.

He took the flying machine off its hook and thrust his skinny legs into what had been, until recently, his second-best pair of trousers (now fireproofed). They were padded around the seat with a layer of foam for comfort. He snapped the suspenders over his shoulders and moved into the middle of the workshop.

At this point, Otto went berserk. If anyone, human or animal, had been watching him, they would have feared for his sanity. Otto heaved his body again and again at the window, willing Bartleby to stop what he was doing and look up. Like some feathery fortune-teller, he could see the disaster that was about to unfold.

Performing a test flight inside the workshop? Bartleby was supposed to initiate takeoff from the wooden launchpad they had built *behind* the workshop! Had the Old Man lost his marbles?

Old Man Bartleby hadn't lost his marbles. He was simply too excited to take the usual precautions. He made some minor alterations to the jet nozzles on the industrial-sized canisters of pressurized hydrogen peroxide, which were attached to the carbon fiber molded harness around the circumference of the pants (unscientifically known as the waist). Then he seized the hand controls he and Otto had constructed out of lightweight aluminum.

"At least put on your safety helmet!" screamed Otto, unable to tear his eyes away from the impending catastrophe.

Bartleby did not put on his safety helmet. His safety helmet was the farthest thing from his mind. He closed his eyes, envisioning himself lifting off the ground and sailing toward the clouds. He shivered at the thought of seeing Ida Valley spread beneath him like a quilt. He would fly—not exactly winging through the sky like his beloved corvids, but alongside them, at least!

Then he took a deep breath and turned the throttle on the right-hand grip, releasing massive blasts of air that thrust him up, up, up. Oh, glory be—the flying machine worked! It worked beautifully! Bartleby soared into the air, doing several loop-de-loops without even meaning to!

Up and up he flew, all the way to the ceiling. If only Otto could see him now! If only—

If only what happened next . . . didn't. But it *did*

happen, just as Otto knew it would. Bartleby bashed his cranium on a rafter and dropped back to the floor. Wisps of compressed air shrouded his body in foggy tendrils. When they evaporated and the dust settled, Otto saw the Old Man lying in a fragile heap, as helpless as a baby raven fallen from its nest.

· 6 ·

You Had Me at Hello

"Ladies and gentlemen, start your engines! *Vroom vroom!*" Miss Furbish pretended to rev up the engine of her invisible motorcycle.

Pippa looked away in embarrassment. *Soooo typical,* she thought. Miss Furbish always forgot she was teaching fifth graders and not little kids.

Still, Pippa was mildly excited about the assignment, which was to make a word mosaic. Everyone had forty-five minutes to write about a memory using words in a way that was creative.

Pippa fished around her vast reservoir of memories involving Otto. After all, she'd known him since he was a clumsy, blue-eyed baby. Pippa tilted her head and counted backward. She'd been seven years old and having a rough time. A really rough time. Otto had been her one bright spot in those days.

She remembered the feeling of Otto's heart beating when she'd cupped him in her hands. She would sit against a wall in Mr. Doyle's workshop and let Otto wobble up and down her outstretched legs. His claws made tiny indentations in her thighs, but they never hurt, the way a person might expect. In fact, she loved the way each of his toes felt on her skin. Every sharp pinprick was a distraction. They helped her not to think about losing her dad.

"Oh my gosh," she muttered under her breath. Losing her dad! Why did people talk about it that way? It wasn't as if she and Mom had gone grocery shopping and accidentally left Dad in the frozen-food aisle. Pippa hadn't misplaced him, like some overdue library book or sunglasses. People lost wallets and backpacks. They lost socks in the laundry. But nobody "lost" their dad.

If anyone was lost, thought Pippa, *it was me.*

It reminded her of the time at Disneyland when she got separated from her parents. How had it even happened? She couldn't say for sure. But before she knew it, she'd been swept along by a crowd of strangers, and Mom and Dad were nowhere to be seen. She wondered if she should go back to the ride they'd just been on, but she couldn't remember which one it was, or where. Everything that had been new and enticing now seemed sinister. The sidewalk felt slanted and menacing under her sandals, as if it were trying to trip her. She grew dizzy. Her breath came in gulps, and her skin was cold. Just as she opened her mouth to scream, they found her. Dad picked her up in his arms. "Where'd you go, Pipsqueak?" he teased her.

"I don't know where I went, because I was lost!" she yelled.

It was the most scared she'd ever been, until a few years later, when she and Mom "lost" Dad forever. She *still* felt that way, if you want to know the truth, only now it was just once in a while, instead of every day.

Pippa sketched an outline of the raven onto her drawing paper. It was a large sheet, the nice kind, so she had room to be expansive. She showed Otto to his greatest advantage. In Pippa's opinion, this was at the moment of landing, when his prodigious wings were still outstretched.

"Prodigious," she said, loud enough so that Roberto, who sat across the table, looked up.

"That's a good word," said Roberto.

"It *is* a good word," said Pippa.

You definitely didn't want to get on the wrong side of Otto's wings. She detailed the primary feathers— the pinions—shading each one with her pencil until it was perfect.

Pippa, did you know that a raven has seventeen pinion feathers, whereas a crow has just sixteen? Why, the difference between a crow and a raven is only a matter of a pinion! This was Mr. Doyle's best joke, and boy, did he tell it a lot. (For the record, if you really want to tell them apart, you have to look at their backsides. Crows spread their tail feathers into the shape of a fan. A raven's tail feathers come to more of a point.)

Pippa tapered Otto's tail feathers into a stylish wedge. She darkened his eye, which, like all ravens', had turned black. His claws, adorably prickly as a baby, were now awe-inspiring talons, and she did them justice.

"What's your flashbart of?" asked Roberto.

"My what?" Pippa asked.

"Your flashbart. It's when you make art out of a flashback." He stood up slightly in his chair and leaned forward to take a look. "Oh," he said, unsurprised. He sat back down and held up his paper for Pippa to see. "I'm not quite the flashbartist that you are."

Pippa couldn't argue with that. "You just covered your paper with zzzzzz's."

"I know," said Roberto. "I'm flashbarting a time I took a nap."

That made Pippa laugh. She looked up at the clock. There were twenty minutes left. Biting her lip in concentration, Pippa began to write. Her tight, compact sentences followed the inner contours of her sketch. Then, in concentric circles that got smaller and smaller, she used her words to fill in Otto's body.

I collect twigs and grass and line the basket of my bike. Today, I'm taking you for your first ride. When Mr. Doyle puts you down, we're amazed at how much you've grown. You barely fit! You sit up straight and turn your head left and right as I pedal around the block as fast as I can. You climb out of the basket onto my handlebars. You are so excited. When we get back to my yard, I stop but you don't. You spread your wings and push off. You fly all the way to the mailbox! I freeze like a statue. My eyes get hot like they always do right before I start to cry. What if you keep going? But then you fly back and put your claw on my hand, and you say—

She had reached the middle of her picture, where Otto's heart might be. There was just enough room for the last word. With a flourish of her pencil, Pippa printed the letters h-e-l-l-o.

7

What We've Got Here
Is Failure to Communicate

Back at the workshop, Otto sat on the windowsill, stunned. The Old Man had just taken things to a whole new level of recklessness.

Of course, Otto had witnessed plenty of accidents. He'd even had a few himself. Inventing things was a risky business. Danger went with the territory. He and Bartleby had caused explosions, inhaled fumes, and built a person-sized pneumatic tube that had malfunctioned pretty spectacularly. And Bartleby had been trying to fly for years. The experiments were many, the setbacks regular.

This isn't his first time at the rodeo, Otto reassured himself. He'd seen the Old Man throw caution to the wind before, and he'd see it again. Now there was little he could do except wait for him to wake up. If experience was anything to go by, it would take about an hour. He decided to fly home in the meantime and see if there was anything Lucille needed.

But first, and against his better judgment, he doubled back around the neighborhood and passed over the park, revisiting the scene of Marla's crime. He recalled her insulting salute, and his anger returned with a vengeance. In fact, it had multiplied greatly.

He wouldn't stand for it. He couldn't stand for it.

By the time Otto reached his nest, he was seething with fury. He opened the door with a bang. Startled, Lucille stopped turning the egg mid-crank.

"What's up?" she said. "You seem upset."

"Oh, do I?" asked Otto, stomping over to the couch and sitting down. "Do I? You know that squirrel Marla?"

"Not really," said Lucille. "I mean, I know who she is, but we don't socialize."

Otto looked at her sharply. Was she teasing him again? Of course ravens and squirrels didn't socialize. The idea was ridiculous.

"Marla," he said, "rankles my rump."

Then he described her theft of the peanuts.

"She was out of line," said Lucille. "I don't blame you for being mad. *I'd* be mad. But that can't be the only thing that's got your tail feathers in a twist."

Otto paused. His wife was a perceptive raven, and very little escaped her attention. It was useless trying to hide much from her. And yet he couldn't bring himself to tell her where he'd been that morning—in fact, where he went most mornings. He couldn't tell her what Bartleby had done.

Why do you spend so much time with the Old Man? she'd asked him once. *Do you think you owe him something?* That was fair enough. After all, Bartleby had scooped Otto off the forest floor when he'd fallen from his parents' nest, bald and ugly as a gargoyle. The Old Man had resuscitated him with bits of bacon, not to mention pineapple juice administered with an eyedropper. He had saved Otto's life.

It's not a matter of owing him, Otto had said.

Otto knew himself best when he was in the work-shop. He had fantastic ideas there. He loved science and he loved inventing things. Plus, it wasn't easy being top bird in Ida Valley, and when he was in the workshop, he didn't worry so much about managing the neighborhood. Most of all, he didn't worry about what life would be like after the egg hatched.

Since he didn't know how to say any of these things to Lucille, it was easier to say nothing at all.

Lucille finished turning the crank, and the egg rolled smoothly to the other side of its box. Her shoulders ached. She felt like she'd been chained to the incubator forever and a day. "What did you bring us for lunch, dear?"

Otto seemed baffled by the question. Lunch? How could his wife think about lunch at a time like this? Then he looked sheepish. He sighed with regret. He studied his feet, shamefaced.

"I forgot about lunch," he finally admitted.

This was turning into a truly wretched morning.

"You forgot about lunch!" said Lucille. She was easygoing, usually, but her patience was wearing thin. "I have an idea. Why don't you fly to the dump and hang out with your buddies for a while? You haven't seen them in a couple of days."

"That's because they're idiots," said Otto.

"They're not idiots!" said Lucille. "You need friends, Otto! Go to the dump! Please! And for cawing out loud, bring me back something to eat!"

8

This Place Is a Dump

The town dump was a glorious place for corvids, who tended to be open-minded about what did and did not constitute food. For Ida Valley's jays, rooks, nutcrackers, magpies, crows, and jackdaws, the dump was heaven on earth. It was an endless smorgasbord of meals. It was a pungent paradise.

And food wasn't its only attraction, either. The

dump was just fun. Mounds of reeking waste were piled higher than houses. A crow could ski down those slopes for hours on nothing more than the lid of a coffee can. Epic games of hide-and-seek were routine, and so was capture the flag, using discarded socks or neckties. Kick the can had recently fallen out of favor after a young blue jay was hit in the eye with a bottle cap. But it was still played when parents weren't watching.

Otto approached the dump from the east, gliding on a warm current of air as he searched for familiar faces. He was an outstanding aviator and could even fly upside down, although he rarely did so. If other ravens could turn a somersault in the sky (and they could), Otto could turn three somersaults. But what was the point of that? He had nothing to prove. He soared in wide circles until he spotted Crouton, easy to pick out of a crowd because he had the fattest head of any crow Otto had ever met.

"Otto P. Nudd!" shouted Crouton as Otto landed nearby. "The one and only! He graces us with his presence! Nuddy's Buddies rejoice!"

This was met with hoots of merriment from the

rest of the gang. They often referred to themselves as Nuddy's Buddies because they suspected it annoyed Otto, which it did.

Otto ignored Crouton and jumped onto a broken chair, glancing around the dump while he folded his wings against his body.

"Looking good, Ottoman," said Fumbles, dropping the brown stalk of celery he'd been toying with. Fumbles, a smallish crow, was missing a few toes on his left foot.

Otto ignored him, too.

"Long time no see you," offered Jacque.

Otto acknowledged this with a quick nod. For a jackdaw, Jacque was interesting, although sometimes it was hard to understand his French Canadian accent. He'd had the misfortune of getting blown off course during an annual migration, and now lived by himself in a chimney. Jacque had a cosmopolitan frame of mind that was sorely lacking at the dump. On the other hand, sometimes he could be just as dumb as everyone else.

"Yeah, it's been, like, weeks," said Bandit.

"It's been two days," Otto said.

Bandit assumed an attitude of indifference. He

twirled the diamond ring he wore on his ankle like a bracelet, making it sparkle in the sunlight. Otto looked away in disgust. Somewhere in Ida Valley, there was a woman who was heartbroken because a magpie had managed to filch her wedding ring. Yes, if it wasn't nailed down, Bandit would steal it. Such was the nature of a magpie.

"So how's the missus?" asked Crouton.

"And ze little *oeuf*?" added Jacque. (Otto's French was limited, but he had long ago deduced that *oeuf* meant "egg," and he was correct.)

"How's the *big oeuf*?" cawed Fumbles. "That's what I wanna know!"

"The big *oeuf*! The big *oeuf*!" giggled Bandit. Then it became too much for him, and he collapsed on the ground, howling with laughter.

Otto shook his head. "You're the big *oeuf*," he muttered to no one in particular.

What was he doing here, anyway? And why *was* his *oeuf* so outrageously huge? Were he and Lucille about to hatch a monster? Exactly what was going to come out of that egg in a few days? *Buck up,* he told himself. *At least you* have *a missus and an* oeuf, *which is more than any of these clowns can say.*

That was true. There was no denying that Otto had achieved quite a lot for such a young bird.

Ravens grow up at an astonishing speed. All corvids do, especially compared to humans. If human parents shoved their one-year-old out the door and made him sleep in the yard, they'd get a visit from the police. But corvid parents do it all the time and nobody says a thing! A two-year-old toddler can't brush her own teeth, but a two-year-old corvid has to find all her own food. While three-year-old humans are busy falling off their tricycles, a three-year-old corvid is ready to get married and settle down. Any normal corvid, at least.

Nuddy's Buddies were not normal. They were the opposite of normal, in Otto's opinion. They spent their days at the dump, eating whatever they could get their claws on and laughing like a pack of hyenas. They were irresponsible. They didn't have jobs. They didn't even have girlfriends, and that included Bandit, who was (Otto had to admit) good-looking when he kept his beak shut.

A bunch of losers was what they were, to Otto P. Nudd's way of thinking. Social rejects. Of course, he'd had a hideous morning and wasn't in the mood to be kind. A better way of putting it was that Crouton, Fumbles, Jacque, and Bandit were late bloomers. But any way you sliced it, they were way behind schedule.

Otto watched sourly as Crouton hacked a blueberry muffin into large chunks. The dump often served up muffins that were factory seconds for one reason or another, but were still quite nice. That is, if you could get one down your gullet. Often, they were too dried out to be edible. But Crouton had found a way around that problem. He simply floated the things in whatever dank puddle of water he could find until they were rehydrated. Otto assumed that was how he'd acquired his nickname, unless his parents had been such numskulls that they'd actually called their son Crouton. In any case, Crouton had solved the problem of stale muffins, and was duly famous for it.

"Not exactly rocket science, though," said Otto under his breath.

Jacque turned a quizzical white eye to Otto. "A dark cloud hangs over you, *mon ami*. What is ze problem?" he asked.

Otto shook his head. How could he even begin

to explain it? He most certainly wasn't about to tell them about this morning's incident.

"How goes ze work with Bartleboo?" Jacque probed.

"Bartleby," corrected Otto.

"Bartleby, Shmartleby," said Fumbles. "Whatcha cookin' up these days with the Old Man?"

Otto's friends knew he and Bartleby often toiled together in the workshop behind Bartleby's house. *But,* reflected Otto, *knowing things and understanding them are two different balls of wax.*

"I don't think I could put it in terms you could fathom," he said.

"Maybe," said Crouton, "you could use real simple words. Like, for example, 'perpendicular.'"

This brought cackles of glee from Nuddy's Buddies. Once, long ago, it had gotten out that the P. in Otto P. Nudd stood for Perpendicular. It was the best joke any of them had ever heard. No other joke even came close. If they were stranded on a desert island and could only bring one joke, it would be Otto's middle name.

"Perpendicular," choked Bandit, trying to catch his breath.

"Shmirpendicular," added Fumbles.

Otto waited for them to pipe down. "That's right," he said. "Get it all out of your systems."

"Sorry, Otto," said Crouton falsely. "We're listening."

Oh, what's the point? Otto asked himself. On the other hand, what else was there to talk about?

"He wants to fly," he heard himself say. "Bartleby wants to fly."

"Of course he does," Crouton responded. "That goes without saying."

Who wouldn't want to soar through the air? Naturally, any human inventor, given enough time, would attempt flight. It just made sense, especially to a bird. No explanation was required.

"It's not that simple," Otto said. "People have been trying to fly for centuries, but the mechanics of flight are so complicated . . . you have to figure out airflow, thrust, stability, control. . . ."

"Baloney," said Fumbles. "I haven't figured any of that stuff out, and I'm great at flying!"

"You're great at flying because you have wings," explained Otto. "What would you do if you woke up tomorrow without any?"

"Without any what?" asked Fumbles.

"Without any wings, you dope," Otto said. "If you didn't have any wings, you'd drop out of the sky like a lump of clay."

Bandit spread his wings into black-and-white fans that shimmered with hints of blue and green. They were stunning, and he knew it. He ruffled his primary feathers for effect. "So the Old Man makes himself a pair of wings, and ta-da! He flies!"

"Put those things away," said Otto, squelching any feelings of jealousy. If Bandit was handsome, he was also a ding-a-ling. "We've made plenty of artificial wings, and they never quite work. The most Bartleby can do is glide down to the ground. But he can't get any altitude."

"Alti-what?" asked Fumbles.

"Altitude," repeated Otto. "He can come down, but he can't go up, no matter how hard he flaps. That's not flying."

"No it ain't," said Crouton.

"However . . . ," Otto began. "However . . ."

He looked at Crouton, Fumbles, Bandit, and Jacque, who had suddenly become very quiet. They even leaned toward him a little, showing an unusual interest in what he was saying. Should he tell them what he and Bartleby were attempting to do? Were they worthy of his confidence? Even Fumbles seemed genuinely curious. Otto made up his mind.

"However," he said, "I think we've found a way to launch a person off the ground. As of this morning, we have a prototype!"

"A proto-what?" asked Fumbles.

"A model of the apparatus!" explained Otto.

"The appa-what?" asked Fumbles.

"For Pete's sake, Fumbles," said Crouton. "They invented a doohickey."

"But what it is, zis doohickey?" Jacque asked.

Otto tried to contain his excitement. "We reinforced a pair of Bartleby's trousers and bonded them to canisters of compressed gas, which, when punctured, will—"

Crouton interrupted him. "Hold on. Do you mean you put rockets in his pants?"

"Yes, essentially," said Otto.

"Are you saying you invented flying pants?"

Nuddy's Buddies froze in place as they considered

the comic implications—the downright hilarity—of flying pants. For a minute, nobody said anything. Then Bandit broke the silence.

"Pants," he said.

It was too much. They crowed with joy. Fumbles and Crouton pounded each other on the back, transported with elation. Tears streamed down Bandit's face as he wept in gratitude for the richness of such a joke. Jacque tried to control himself but gave up, doubling over with mirth until he fell sideways onto a pile of wet cardboard.

It went on and on.

Otto looked at them in disgust, part of which he reserved for himself. He should have known better. How often had he shared an important idea with these guys, only to watch them turn it into a farce? It was pearls before swine, every single time.

I'm a fool, he lamented. *A real grade-A sucker. First Marla, then the Old Man, and now this. I'm never telling them anything again. Ever.*

He remembered that Lucille still needed lunch and cast his eyes around the dump. There was always something worth eating if you looked closely. Sure enough, he spied a trampled pizza box poking out of the trash, not far from where Nuddy's Buddies were whooping it up. He marched over and pulled it free with his beak, opening it to reveal several well-ripened slices of pepperoni pizza.

Bingo, thought Otto. *Lucille's favorite.*

Then he saw something else, a twisted spiral of steel wire half-buried in the rubbish. He hooked his beak around it and yanked until, dislodged, it revealed itself to be a Slinky. A Slinky in very good working order.

Otto played around with it, holding one end down with his foot and stretching the other end as far as it would go before letting it snap back. *Sproing!* He did this for several minutes, evaluating the possibilities. It was a child's toy, sure. But it was so much more than that. He contemplated the silvery coils from this angle and that, until an idea formed in his brain—a breathtaking vision of revenge, a perfect serving of justice.

"Yes," he said. "Oh, yes."

With a slice of pizza in one claw and the Slinky dangling from the other, he rose from the pile of garbage like a vengeful god, and flew home.

Someone was about to get her comeuppance.

9

Gravity Will Always Bring You Down

Otto all but threw the pizza in Lucille's direction before sprinting to Pippa's backyard, where he dropped the Slinky at the base of the bird feeder. He looked up, examining its structure. It was just as he'd thought: a simple pole hammered into the ground that extended six feet into the air. A gracefully curving bracket at the top stuck out over the grass and ended in a hook. From the hook dangled the glass hopper that Pippa had filled that morning. It brimmed with premium birdseed.

Marla hasn't been here yet, he thought. *It's not too late.*

As a rule, Otto didn't bother with Pippa's bird feeder. He didn't care who helped themselves to the sunflower chips, cracked corn, millet, and raisins that poured out of its little circular slots onto a tray. The birdseed was for the small fry of the neighborhood, those lesser birds whose nutritional habits were none of Otto's concern. He knew full well that squirrels raided the bird feeder and that among those squirrels, Marla was notorious for raiding it the hardest. But the whole thing was trivial in the larger context of Otto's life. Until today.

Otto snipped one end of the Slinky and hitched the wire around the bottom of the bird feeder. Working deliberately, he threaded coil after coil around the pole until he reached the other end of the Slinky. Now it girded the bird feeder like a thick belt.

The easy part was over. Otto thought for a bit about how to accomplish the rest. He needed to move the Slinky all the way up the pole, and there was no straightforward way to do it. Brute strength and agility, he decided. Fortunately, Otto had plenty of both. He hoisted himself onto the pole, grabbing it in his claws and turning himself around until his black head pointed toward the earth.

Otto clamped a wiry loop in his beak and started to back up the pole, tail feathers first. He put one foot behind the other, muscles bulging and straining. Otto dragged the Slinky higher and higher until he arrived at the top. Here, he righted himself and stepped sideways onto the bracket. He stood there, balancing like a gymnast.

Then, in one deft maneuver, he dropped the loop in his beak over the tip of the pole. It caught itself neatly in the crook between the pole and bracket. The rest of the Slinky spiraled down the pole like the long tail of a snake. It stretched out and snapped back for a while, as a Slinky does. Then it came to rest.

Otto flew to the ground and looked up at what he'd done. He tried not to gloat. But a warm, marvelous feeling began to spread through his body. He walked over to the Japanese maple and ducked under its branches. Then he settled in, waiting to see what would happen.

He did not wait long.

Some chickadees landed on the tray under the hopper and pecked daintily at the seeds. They traded gossip for a while, and scattered when a house sparrow joined them. The sparrow, whom Otto knew by sight but not by name, was an unlikable bird—a bully, even. He was used to getting his way at the feeder. But after gobbling up a few sunflower chips, he froze in terror and then flew away as fast as he could.

The sparrow had sensed the presence of a threat. He'd been scared. All bullies fear an even bigger bully—you can count on it. There was movement by a gap in the bottom of the fence separating Pippa's yard from the forest. Otto watched intently. A squirrel emerged from the gap and sauntered over to the bird feeder. By the patches in her scraggly dun-colored coat and the homeliness of her gaunt face, Otto knew her at once.

It was Marla.

Otto breathed harder, relishing what he was about to see.

Like an Olympian, Marla sprang onto the pole. She was fast and a darn good jumper—Otto had to give her that much. She scrambled upward until she reached the lowest coil of the Slinky, which she seized in both paws. Then it happened. With a sudden *whoosh!* and *sproing!* the Slinky stretched out under Marla's weight, and she was flung back to the ground. She lay there in a daze, unsure of what had just happened.

It was one of the most beautiful things Otto had ever witnessed.

Marla made a second pass at the pole, vaulting even higher and climbing even faster. Once again, as soon as she ascended to the bottom of the Slinky and grabbed it, she dropped to the earth like a sack of rocks. She stood up, the picture of bewilderment and disbelief.

Otto's heart swelled with joy. He felt a kind of ecstasy.

Marla backed up eight or nine feet. She blew on her palms and rubbed them together. She cracked her knuckles. She shook out her legs, first the left one and then the right, and rotated her ankles. She rolled her scrawny shoulders. Then she launched herself at the bird feeder, running like the wind. With every ounce of strength she had, Marla hurled herself onto the pole, scaling its height so quickly that her limbs were a blur. When she reached the Slinky, the sheer momentum of her ascent pushed it up and up until she was a mere foot from the top. But the coils could be compressed no further.

Marla released the pole and clutched the Slinky, hoping to shinny up its loops before it expanded one more time. Her failure was stupendous.

In a contest between gravity and a determined squirrel, put your money on gravity. Gravity wins each and every time.

The gravitational force that yanked the squirrel (and the Slinky) back down the pole was merciless. Marla hit the ground with the impact of a small meteorite. She hit it so hard, in fact, that she bounced back up, then hit it again!

Otto gawked at the sight. Never had an invention worked so perfectly. It had, in fact, exceeded his expectations. He replayed the image of Marla being lobbed from the bird feeder over and over, and his happiness was complete. He cawed with jubilation.

Marla rose to her feet with some effort, holding her head in her paws. She wobbled a bit but then steadied herself. Turning gingerly to the source of the laughter, she spotted Otto under the Japanese maple. Their eyes met.

Otto stopped cawing. He knew today's lesson would not be lost on Marla. There would be no more thieving. His authority would be recognized, and she would behave like a law-abiding squirrel. He had nothing more to say.

Marla, on the other hand, had a few choice words for Otto. They were the following:

"This. Is. War."

10

Play It Again, Pippa

While Otto and Marla were busy becoming mortal enemies, Pippa wandered around the schoolyard like a zombie. So did all the other kids. They shuffled in small groups across the patchy grass behind the school building. There was no shouting or laughing or any of the other noises that (once upon a time) used to identify recess. It was the low point of everyone's day.

Bored, bored, outta my gourd, Pippa chanted to herself.

She drifted over to the corner of the yard where Roberto was talking to a group of fourth and fifth graders. The way he was gesticulating with his hands, pausing only to push his glasses up his nose, made it seem like he was communicating something vitally important.

I don't care if he's saying the alphabet, thought Pippa. *It's better than nothing.*

But Roberto wasn't saying the alphabet. He was giving a history lesson.

"Back in the day," Roberto was saying, "kids looked forward to recess. If you asked them what their favorite class was, they used to say 'recess' every time."

"Sounds like an urban legend," said Julia.

"What's an urban legend?" asked Malcolm.

"A story that's a lie," said Julia. Sometimes Julia could be brutal.

"Nope, it's completely true," continued Roberto, unruffled. "Recess was fun. See that scratched-up piece of dirt over there?"

The kids looked in the direction Roberto pointed.

"That's where the seesaw used to be, a long time ago. But a second grader fell off it and knocked his front teeth out."

"Baby teeth or permanent teeth?" asked Moses E.

"Permanent," said Roberto conclusively. "The next day, the seesaw was gone. Then a kid climbed on top of the monkey bars next to where the seesaw had been. He stayed there all day, until the school called his parents. But he still wouldn't come down, so the school had to call the fire department."

"No way," said Moses A.

"Oh, yes," said Roberto. "They took the boy *and* the monkey bars away. And that's not all."

He told the tale of a metal slide with countless steps rising above the treetops. Its long, sinewy surface gleamed like a mirror, reflecting the sun so brilliantly that you had to squint just to look at it. One day, the slide gave a third grader's leg such a blistering burn that she'd had to go to the nurse's office.

"Whose fault was that?" demanded Julia. "Everyone knows you don't go down a metal slide on a sunny day wearing shorts."

"I agree," Roberto conceded. "But they got rid of the slide, just like that." He snapped his fingers.

A gloomy pall settled over the children.

Roberto was unrelenting. "Then they outlawed the games," he said.

"Which games?" asked Evie.

"All of them," said Roberto. "Marbles are a choking hazard, so they banned marbles. Dodgeball is, like, open season on the slow kids, so they said it was off-limits. Kickball makes you choose sides against each other, so *adiós,* kickball. Don't even get me started with Simon Says."

"What's wrong with Simon Says?" asked Moses A.

"Do you know how confusing that game is for kids named Simon?" Roberto asked. "They banned Simon Says forever."

"And jumping rope?" asked Evie.

"Take a wild guess," said Roberto.

"It's just so incredibly dumb," mourned Malcolm. He looked at the schoolyard with deep sorrow. So did everyone else. "There's nothing left. They took away all the games."

"Not all the games," said Pippa. She was surprised to hear herself speak.

"What are you talking about?" asked Julia.

Pippa stepped forward until she was in the middle of the group. An idea was forming in her mind, urgent and compelling. "I know a game we can play that's way more fun than dodgeball or kickball or any of that stuff."

"Let me guess," said Julia. "Does it have anything to do with crows?"

This caused some snickering among the other children. Pippa's love of corvids was well known to her classmates, and deemed quite peculiar.

"Yeah, it has something to do with crows," said Pippa. "*Dead* crows."

The snickering stopped.

Pippa glanced at Roberto. Would he help her or not? The game hinged on his cooperation—she sensed that clearly. Roberto raised an eyebrow above the rim of his glasses and grinned in a conspiratorial sort of way. He was on board.

"Roberto, you're going first," she said. "Lie down."

Roberto dropped onto the grass immediately.

Pippa continued, "We're going to play a game called Crow Funeral. And in case you're wondering, crows have funerals. In real life."

She could feel the skepticism rolling off her classmates like waves. It was irksome, to say the least.

"When a crow, um, bites the dust," she said, choosing her words carefully, "all the other crows walk around him. They do it for hours. They walk in a ring around their friend."

"Interesting, but hard to believe," observed Roberto from where he lay on the ground.

"Then look it up," said Pippa severely. "It's true. Also, you're the first crow, so start acting like it."

Roberto, surprised and delighted by Pippa's unaccustomed bossiness, tried to look lifeless.

"It's not fair," Julia said. "Why does Roberto get to be the first crow?"

"We're all crows," Pippa explained. "And it's totally fair. Everyone gets a turn. Here's the rule: whoever says the best thing about their friend gets to move to the middle of the ring."

"This is just weird," said Julia.

"No it isn't," argued Roberto, raising himself on one elbow. "It's what you do at funerals—you say nice things about the dearly departed. You tell stories about them. That's what we did at my abuelita's funeral."

"Your who?" asked Moses A.

"My grandma," clarified Roberto. "We said all the things we were going to miss about her."

That's what we did, too, thought Pippa. *Except I didn't even know how many things I was going to miss about Dad. Not even a fraction.*

"But what if we can't think of the best thing to say?" asked Malcolm. "Or anything at all?"

"We've known each other forever, Malcolm," said Pippa with exaggerated sufferance. "You'll come up with something."

The children weighed the options. Was this better than doing nothing until the bell rang? There was only one way to find out. They made a space around Roberto and began to walk in a circle.

Pippa went first. "I loved the way Roberto always whispered when he had something important to say. The more important it was, the harder it was to hear him."

Then it was Julia's turn. Not to be outdone by Pippa, she dug deep. "When we were in soccer and it was Roberto's turn for snacks, he always brought the saltiest pretzels. They made me so thirsty. I miss those days."

Moses A. went next. "Roberto was the first one of us to learn how to tie his shoelaces. That's when I found out how smart he was. That's when I knew."

Moses E. followed Moses A. "There was this one time Roberto made me laugh so hard that I pulled a muscle in my stomach and I had to stay home from school. Except it turned out I actually had appendicitis, and I had to go to the hospital." He smiled wistfully. "I always had a gut feeling about that kid."

"He was great at drawing self-portraits?" said Evie, who ended every observation with a question mark. "He could even do noses? And not just triangles with two holes for the nostrils? They looked real? He promised he would show me how to do it someday, but I guess it's too late now?" Her grievance trailed off, to be addressed at a future date.

Malcolm followed Evie. "There was this one time I was feeling really bad about my Halloween costume because, you know, it was the worst costume in history. I wanted to be Spider-Man, but my mom made me be a carrot. Roberto said I looked funny and that he was rooting for me."

Each of the kids got to be the crow in the middle of the ring. They shared fond memories and spoke of good times together. A few of them flapped their wings, imitating a crow's careful, jerking motions. When the bell finally rang, they filed back into the building with reluctance. It had been the best recess any of them could remember.

"That game was awesome," whispered Roberto as they took their seats. "Let's play it again sometime."

"Definitely," said Pippa.

11

WWBD?

Marla's threat did not especially worry Otto. He despised war, believe it or not. As a pillar of the community, he led with his brains, not his brawn. *Of course,* as he told himself, *if she brings a fight to my door, she will certainly find me home.* But in all likelihood, Marla had learned her lesson. He watched her squeeze under the back fence, and considered the matter closed.

It was time to wing it to the workshop, where the Old Man surely had recovered his senses and was waiting to let him in. Together, they would review what had gone wrong during the initial test of their flying machine, and prepare for a second trial.

Otto flew over the fence between Pippa's and Bartleby's houses, landing on the sill of the workshop window. He flattened the side of his face against the glass, trying to see through the thick dust that spackled the window on both sides. Bartleby came into focus, twisted limply on the cement floor.

Otto tried to caw, but no sound came out. His beak hung open with shock. This was the possibility he had refused to entertain until now. It was a fiasco beyond his wildest imaginings. Were his eyes playing tricks on him? He looked again. Bartleby lay still. Otto couldn't tell whether he was even breathing.

The raven felt his world darken and wither around him. His rib cage constricted, and his legs became as stiff and brittle as twigs. His feet grew cold, and he lost his grip on the sill. Tipping backward, he fell from its edge in a rigid swoon. Only force of habit saved him—his wings flapped instinctively, and he was carried back up into the air, where he flew in tight, mindless circles.

What do I do now? What do I do now? What do I do now? he asked himself, the question pulsing in his ears like the pounding of his own heart. At last, he returned to the window and mashed himself against the glass so hard, he could feel bruises forming under his feathers. This seemed to help him concentrate.

Years ago, Bartleby had installed an alarm button inside his workshop. It was a big one—about the size of a grapefruit—and it summoned the paramedics. The word EMERGENCY was stamped into its surface, as well as a white cross. It was one of the few truly sensible things he had ever done. To the best of Otto's knowledge, nobody had ever pushed the button.

Now it glowed like a red eye, watching him, promising to send help if he could just get inside and press it.

Otto stared back, mesmerized. That was it! The button! He had to get in there and press the button.

If this isn't an emergency, he thought, *then my name isn't Otto P. Nudd.*

He squared his shoulders and prepared to spring into action. But nothing happened. He just sat there like a bump on a log. It's astoundingly difficult to come up with a plan when you feel that every minute brings you closer to the brink of disaster. This was the cruel situation Otto found himself in.

Think, Otto, think! he commanded himself. *WWBD?*

WWBD? was shorthand for "What would Bartleby do?" It was by posing this question to himself that Otto frequently came up with some of his most brilliant ideas. *WWBD?* he repeated. The letters became a mantra. *WWBD? WWBD?*

Two words popped into his mind:

(1) *mechanical*

(2) *advantage*

When Bartleby was in a pinch, he applied mechanical advantage! And that's precisely what Otto intended to do.

12

Everything You Always Wanted to Know About Mechanical Advantage but Were Afraid to Ask

You're clever and astute. You have a perfect understanding of mechanical advantage. You've studied it endlessly, and if there's one thing you know, it's this: *mechanical advantage is how much help you get from a machine.* No doubt about it.

But in case there's the smallest scintilla of uncertainty (and I'm not saying there is), let's do a quick experiment. Imagine, if you will, a field mouse sitting on a seesaw.

Wait a minute, you say indignantly. Why should this mouse (whose name is Wilma) be allowed to have a seesaw when Pippa and her classmates aren't? That's not fair.

Correct. It *isn't* fair. But thank goodness Wilma has one anyway, because it's a superb example of a machine that uses mechanical advantage!

But seesaws aren't machines, you protest.

Ah, that's where you're wrong. A seesaw *is* a machine, albeit a simple one. And Wilma is sitting on it. She isn't having much fun because she's all by herself, and that's no good when it comes to seesaws. She waits patiently for someone to come along and play with her.

Lo and behold, who should pass by but her good friend Raúl the guinea pig. Now Wilma can have some fun!

Hold on, you object with vehemence. This won't work. Raúl outweighs Wilma by a factor of thirty, at least! In her wildest dreams, Wilma will never be able to lift her portly playmate off the ground, let alone go up and down and up and down and up and down. Right?

Incorrect! Wilma and Raúl can sit together on a seesaw with the greatest of ease, and they often do! Raúl just needs to scoot closer to the middle of the seesaw—the point where it tips back and forth. That part is called the "fulcrum." If Raúl sits close enough to the fulcrum, his bite-sized buddy can lift him up without breaking a sweat.

In other words, the seesaw helps Wilma do something she can't accomplish with her own puny muscles. It turns her into a Wonder Mouse. And it does this with—you guessed it—mechanical advantage!

As if that weren't amazing enough, the seesaw can give Raúl some superpowers, too. On his own (if Wilma gives him permission), Raúl can lift his minuscule friend off the ground and throw her up into the air. It's no big deal. It's nothing to write home about. But let's put them back on the seesaw and reverse their positions. Let's suppose that this time, Wilma scoots *toward* the fulcrum while Raúl moves *away* from it, closer to the end of the seesaw. Let's say he sits down as hard as he can. What will happen to Wilma then?

She'll be tossed through the sky like a beanbag, that's what. She'll be hurled into outer space, practically. She'll go ballistic. (Please don't try this on the playground—it really hurts.)

The thing you need to know is this: mechanical advantage turns an ordinary animal into a super-hero. It's just sensational.

And Otto wanted a lot of it, fast.

13

Otto Starts Inventing Stuff Like Crazy

Now wave after wave of inspiration flooded Otto's brain.

He first thought of using a humble lever. Levers were positively loaded with mechanical advantage. Hadn't Bartleby often claimed that with a long-enough lever, he could move the earth out of its orbit? What if Otto cobbled together some sort of massive crowbar? He could pry the workshop's roof from its walls, popping it off like the lid of a can of paint.

But how would he construct a lever that was long enough for a job like that? He'd need days and days to assemble something of that scale.

"This is no time for theoretical gobbledygook," he scolded himself savagely. "WWBD? WWBD?"

A rudimentary catapult came to mind, the machine used by the Romans to toss large bags of bees at their enemies. Or was it clay pots full of venomous snakes? Or corpses bloated with gases and disease? Oh, it didn't matter! The question was whether he could build a catapult with enough power to fling a rock through the window and break the glass. He could. He knew he could.

Except that he needed tools—the very tools that were locked inside the workshop, with Bartleby.

How about a battering ram that could pound through a wall? A huge crossbow that could shoot an arrow through the window? Some kind of slingshot?

Otto groaned with frustration. Again, inventions required tools. They required time. He had neither.

In theory, there was scads of *potential* mechanical

advantage. But in reality, the tools to unleash it were trapped inside Bartleby's workshop. This seemed grossly unfair.

What if he managed to chop down one of the trees that towered behind the workshop, felling it in such a way as to punch a hole through the roof? On the other hand, what if the same tree crushed Bartleby? No, it was too risky.

How about starting a controlled fire and burning his way into the workshop? Otto considered this briefly before admitting it was his worst idea yet.

"You're not going to WWBD your way out of this one," he croaked to himself.

A horrible realization began to dawn on him. He tried to ignore it, to force one last scheme from his exhausted brain. But there was nothing left. He was well and truly out of ideas. Otto slumped against the window in defeat. If he was going to save Bartleby, he was going to have to ask for help.

But that didn't mean he had to like it.

I'd rather pluck my own tail feathers, he thought bleakly. *Or step on a tack, or swallow a bee. But what choice do I have?*

14

Maybe They're Not Such Nitwits After All

Otto tore himself away from the window and leapt from the sill, his wings slicing through the air like black scimitars. He flew with an urgency he'd never felt before. As soon as he'd acknowledged the dreadful fact that he needed help, an idea had popped into his brain. Speed was everything.

"It'll work," he muttered, scanning the edge of the woods. "It's got to."

There they were, a throng of lesser birds, the non-corvids of Ida Valley.

Until today, Otto's dealings with them had been limited to pointing out the structural defects in their nests.

Why do you waste your time? Lucille would often ask. *They're as dumb as corncobs!*

Otto thought this was harsh but probably accurate. Goldfinches, to take an example, wove their nests so tightly that they could hold water like a cup. This was all well and good until it rained. Then their little chicks, who couldn't swim to save their lives, were in trouble. The goldfinches tried to solve the problem by covering everything with an awning made of leaves. However, Otto favored a small plug hole in the bottom of each nest for speedy drainage.

His advice was not always well received by young mothers, who were quick to show their disdain by lunging and pecking at him.

"There's no way for the water to escape, the way you do it!" said Otto sternly.

"There is! There is!" argued the mothers.

"You'll come home one day and it will be too late!"

insisted Otto. "Your babies will be floating around like corks!"

"No they won't! No they won't!" the mothers shouted, flapping their wings hysterically.

Otto turned his head to the side, presenting the fearsome curve of his mighty beak. "If you haven't fixed your nests by tomorrow, I'll do it for you."

"Go away!" they whimpered. "Go away. . . ."

Otto heckled them until they fell in line.

He visited a number of black-capped chickadees who drilled their nests too close to the ground, and then complained of the damp. "Aim higher, stay drier!" he instructed them. And lately, the wood thrushes had taken to weaving pieces of white paper into their nests, giving them a swanky appearance that Otto found tasteless. "Flashy equals trashy," he admonished. "A paper nest is second-best!"

The nuthatches didn't use enough mud to seal their entrances. The sparrows built their dwellings too close together—a flagrant code violation.

Otto got precious little credit for what he did. In fact, he suspected that the lesser birds resented his advice, but he gave it to them anyway. He was the only bird with the brains to see when things weren't up to snuff. Without him, the neighborhood would come apart at the seams. And now it was their turn to give *him* a little help.

The lesser birds balanced on the seed heads of tall, spiny thistles. They swayed in the warm afternoon breeze, gossiping wildly about anything and everything. The noise was earsplitting. Mostly, they were goldfinches, with a few of the chattier sparrows. This was perfect, as far as Otto was concerned. Goldfinches were the ideal size.

"Listen up, all you lessers," he cawed, landing on a grassy spot where he could be seen and heard by everyone. "There's been an emergency, and I'm going to require your assistance."

The squawking shrank to a low murmuration.

"Require what? Require what?" asked a mustard-colored female. She was immediately echoed by others. "Require? Require?"

"I need your help!" shouted Otto. The words left a bad aftertaste on his tongue.

The birds fell into a shocked silence.

"Our neighbor Bartleby Doyle has suffered an injury, and we need to act fast before it's too late!" Otto cawed. His voice rang with authority.

The lesser birds seemed bewildered. "Suffered a what? A what?" they asked.

Otto spoke slowly. "He's hurt himself badly," he began, "and—"

"Who did?" came a voice from the flock. "Who did? Who?"

"Bartleby Doyle, you nitwit! Pay attention!" Otto snapped. "He lives next to the girl Pippa! Good grief, you can practically see his house from here!"

They fell silent once more, and Otto continued. "Bartleby flew into his ceiling and knocked himself unconscious. Now he's trapped inside—"

"Flew?" shrieked an elderly sparrow. "He flew? The man flew?"

The feverish note in her voice was as contagious as chicken pox. It spread like wildfire through the lesser birds, until the woods reverberated with the word "flew." *"Flew? Flew? Flew?"* The sound filled Otto's ears like the buzzing of locusts.

He looked from bird to bird, incredulous. He could feel the seconds ticking away, every one bringing

Bartleby closer to the brink of disaster. Couldn't they sense how perilous the situation was? Couldn't they grasp the danger the Old Man was in?

"Quiet!" roared Otto.

Silence was restored immediately.

"The next bird who opens his beak is going to regret it," he cawed. "So help me, I will knock your heads together like walnuts if I hear another word!"

No one made so much as a peep.

"My friend is trapped inside his workshop, and the door is locked! There's only one way to get inside the building, and that's through an unused air vent on the roof. It's a pipe, to be precise. I need a few volunteers to squeeze through the pipe!"

There were no volunteers.

"Once you're through the pipe, you'll see a large red button on the wall next to the door. You can't miss it! A large red button! Do you follow what I'm saying?"

He gave the birds a moment to indicate they understood. A few of them stole glances at each other. He pressed on.

"The next part is the most important: you must fling yourselves at the red button until you hear the

alarm. Do you understand? You must fling yourselves at the button as hard as you can, again and
again. Fling yourselves until you manage to alert
the authorities. Flinging is crucial."

A number of the goldfinches tilted their heads
sideways, as if deep in thought. Several of them
closed their eyes in concentration.

Otto repeated himself, enunciating each word
with care. "I need two or three of you to squeeze
through the pipe, enter the workshop, and fling
yourselves at the red button. Now, who's with me?"

He fixed his audience with a piercing stare. The
mustard-colored female slowly raised her wing. She
cleared her throat and addressed him in a tremulous
chirp. "Pipe? Pipe? What is a pipe?"

She looked around to see who shared her confusion. Many did. "And what is 'fling'?" she asked, baffled by the complexity of the word.

A murmur rippled through the lesser birds as
they attempted to make sense of Otto's instructions.
"Fling? Fling? Fl . . . Fl . . . FFFF . . . FFFFF . . ."
The noise swirled around Otto like steam from a tea-
kettle.

"Are you serious?" he asked them. Of course

they were idiots through and through. But he had never encountered this level of obtuseness. "When I say 'fling,' I mean that you must throw yourselves against . . ."

And then he saw it. The mustardy finch turned her face away from him. She looked at her neighbor through slyly lowered lids. The beginnings of a smile teased the corners of her bill. She bounced on her toes ever so slightly, excited by her own cleverness.

The truth dawned on Otto all at once.

Why, she's not confused at all, he thought. *She knows exactly what "fling" means. She's being defiant!*

He was right. They were all defying him.

Otto felt he might choke from rage. For a moment, he forgot about Bartleby Doyle lying on the floor of his workshop. The only thing he wanted to do was kick the lessers all the way from Ida Valley down to Mexico and back again.

"You little twits!" Otto shouted. *"What is 'fling'?* I'll show you what *fling* is. I'll fling you through that pipe myself. I'll fling you so hard, you won't know your beaks from your behinds!"

He ran at them in a blind fury. He would knock them off their perches. He would scatter them like bowling pins. They would think twice before challenging Otto P. Nudd again, that was for sure. This was a lesson they would not soon forget.

But if the lesser birds were anything, they were quick. Off they flew in every direction, disappearing into the woods, laughing, their empty perches bobbing up and down in the sunshine.

15

His Buddies Decline to Fall in Line

"What just happened?" Otto asked. He gaped at the thistles where dozens of lesser birds had been just two seconds ago. Now they'd vanished into thin air. Had he really threatened them with force and charged at them? He, who never sank to violence? He, whose reign over the woods was uncontested and absolute?

Was he having a nightmare?

Instinctively, Otto plucked a feather from his chest. It hurt. He was definitely awake.

Otto swore and yanked the heads off a few late-summer flowers. Then he stopped. If any of the lesser birds were watching (and he was sure they were), it wouldn't do to throw a tantrum. And a tantrum wouldn't help save Bartleby Doyle.

Bartleby Doyle! He'd deal with the goldfinch mutiny later. Right now, he was racing against time. If the lesser birds wouldn't help him, the guys would. Otto headed to the town dump.

Why hadn't he gone to his fellow corvids in the first place? he wondered. *I should have,* he admitted, *but I didn't have a plan. Still don't.* Maybe they could help him come up with a scheme to get into the workshop. Sure, it was a long shot. They were only marginally smarter than the lesser birds, which is to say pretty dense. But you never knew.

Otto sped to the dump and looked for Crouton, Fumbles, Bandit, and Jacque. They were easy to spot: four dark shapes sprawled on top of an ancient yellow school bus. He'd never been so glad to see them.

"Heads up!" he called, diving toward the bus. He came to a skidding halt a few feet away.

They looked at him in surprise. It wasn't like Otto to visit them twice in one day, much less make such an inelegant landing.

"Otto P. Nudd, again!" said Crouton. "To what do we owe the pleasure?"

"Yeah, what gives, Ottoman?" asked Fumbles.

"You are huffing and puffing, *mon ami,*" Jacque observed.

Bandit raised his eyebrows in a way that was both handsome and questioning. "Everything okay?"

Otto shook his head, gasping for air. Finally, he caught his breath. "No," he said, "everything is not okay. There's been an accident. You need to come with me to Bartleby Doyle's workshop right away."

The corvids stared at Otto, agog. This was unprecedented. He'd never invited them to the workshop before. In fact, he'd forbidden them to come within a hundred yards of it.

"Say what?" asked Fumbles dimly.

"There's no time to lose," said Otto. "Come to the workshop and I'll explain everything on the way."

"We're not allowed to go to the workshop," Bandit said. He spoke slowly. The diamond ring on his ankle glittered, refracting the sunlight straight into Otto's eyes. Otto blinked.

"There's no time to lose," he repeated. "Bartleby has flown into the ceiling and knocked himself unconscious!"

"But zis is terrible!" exclaimed Jacque as Otto's words sank in.

"It's worse than terrible," Otto said. "He might be dying. The door is locked. There's no way to get in."

"So whaddya want us to do about it?" asked Crouton.

"I haven't exactly devised a solution yet," Otto hedged, "but I'll have one soon. Probably by the time we get to the workshop, in fact. So let's go."

"Hold your horses," said Crouton, standing up and stretching his wings as if the very concept of being in a hurry was completely foreign to him, which it was. "Go back to the part where you said you don't know what to do."

"I didn't say I didn't know what to do," objected Otto.

"Yeah, you did," said Crouton. "You said you didn't have a solution."

"What I said was that I will have a solution by the time we get to the workshop!" Otto's voice cracked with the strain of trying to stay calm in the face of calamity.

Crouton sat back down. "I'll tell you what. Nuddy's Buddies are gonna stay right here until Otto P. Nudd comes up with a 'solution.'"

He made little air quotes with his wings around the word "solution," as if Otto were incapable of figuring anything out, let alone how to save Bartleby Doyle.

Otto glared at Crouton. The traitor! So this was what it felt like to be stabbed in the back! He'd never trusted Crouton, not for one minute. Never count on a crow with a head the size of a baseball.

"Are you going to sit there and do nothing while the greatest inventor Ida Valley has ever known takes his last breath?" he demanded.

"I never said I was gonna do nothing. I just wanna hear you say that you don't know what to do and that—even though as recently as last week, you told me I was too dumb to peck my way outta a paper bag—you need my help."

"I didn't say that," said Otto. "I'm sure you misunderstood me. As usual."

"You did say it," insisted Crouton. "Those were your exact words. Too dumb to peck my way outta a paper bag, you said."

"Direct quote," said Bandit.

"Too dumb to peck his way out," mumbled Fumbles.

Jacque nodded apologetically. "Your words *exactement*."

"I have no recollection of saying you were too dumb to peck your way out of a paper bag," insisted Otto. "But in any case, could we talk about it after we rescue Bartleby Doyle?"

"Nope. The Old Man's just gonna have to wait until you remember what you said." Crouton paused, and then raised the stakes. "Oh, and until you apologize."

Now Crouton had gone too far. It was hard enough coming to everyone, cap in hand, asking for help. But apologizing for stating the obvious was never, ever, *ever* going to happen.

"You know what?" said Otto in a voice that was as cold as iron. "I'll say I'm sorry when pigs fly."

In spite of themselves, Crouton, Bandit, Fumbles, and Jacque glanced upward, half expecting to see a pig sailing through the air.

"That means never, you morons. Have a nice life in the dump."

Otto left his so-called buddies, in a greater fury than he had ever known.

· 16 ·

A Tiny Crush Is Born

Something curious was unfolding at Ida Valley Elementary. Specifically, it was unfolding in Pippa's classroom, at the very table where Pippa sat.

"Julia," said Roberto, "I brought you something for your birthday."

It was almost the end of the day, when Pippa and her classmates had science. They sat in groups of five, quietly completing their worksheets about the life

101

cycle of moss. Pippa sat with Roberto, Julia, Moses A., and Moses E. in the back of the room. The exhilaration of recess had largely worn off. They had finished their work early and were talking about other things.

"Today isn't my birthday," Julia pointed out.

"Her birthday isn't until next week," said Moses E., who had one of those rare brains that can't forget a birthday even if they try.

"I know her birthday isn't until next week," said Roberto smoothly. "But I brought her something today."

"Is it a present?" asked Pippa.

"What else would it be?" Moses A. asked.

"Just because you give someone something on their birthday doesn't mean it's a present," argued Pippa.

"Again," said Julia, "today isn't my birthday."

"Is it edible?" asked Moses A.

"I wouldn't recommend it," said Roberto. "But I guess if you're really hungry . . ."

This piqued their curiosity, just as Roberto had known it would.

"It's irrelevant," insisted Julia. "Because today's not my birthday."

"I guess you don't want it, then," Roberto said with a shrug. "No biggie."

"Of course she wants it," said Moses E.

Julia looked around the table, wavering. Moses E. was right. She wanted it, whatever it was. "All right, fine," she said.

Roberto smiled indulgently. He reached into his pocket and took out a small white box. Its tastefulness suggested something agreeable inside: a ring, or even a necklace! Pippa, Moses A., and Moses E. leaned across the table for a better view. Julia's eyes sparkled with sudden excitement. Roberto lifted the top from the box, and held it out for all to see.

Inside the box was a thumb.

A thumb.

A bloody, stumpy, undeniably human thumb.

Julia screamed, and so did the Moseses. Kids everywhere dropped their worksheets and rushed to the back of the classroom to see what the excitement was about. Some of them screamed, too, just to join in. Roberto thrust the box into his pocket and leaned back, grinning widely. Victory was his.

Pippa gazed at him in admiration. She had quickly deduced everything, which was this: Roberto had cut a hole in the bottom of the box and its downy layer of cotton. He swabbed the box's interior with a marker or paint, coloring it blood-red. Then he stuck his own thumb through the hole. Oldest trick in the book. But it was convincing. And it was very, very funny.

Of course, there was a price for all this hilarity, and Roberto was going to pay it. As he was escorted out of the classroom by the collar of his shirt, his eyes met Pippa's. He winked at her. And without thinking twice, she winked back.

· 17 ·

Foiled by You-Know-Who

Pippa wasn't the only one having new kinds of feelings. Otto, too, was experiencing something for the first time, and that was self-doubt.

He remembered when his authority was unquestioned. Now there were questions aplenty! For example, why had that horrible squirrel stolen his peanuts right in front of him? And why had the Old Man shut him out of the workshop and tested their invention without him? Why had the lesser birds ignored his commands and mocked him? Why hadn't his buddies seen the trouble he was in and come with him, instead of being such a bunch of jerks?

These were things that simply wouldn't have happened to Otto P. Nudd, bird for the ages. But that was a different raven, from a different time.

Honestly, he'd stopped being that raven the day Lucille had laid their egg. It was going to hatch sooner or later, and when it did, whatever came out of it was going to call him Dad. Otto didn't have a clue how he was supposed to act. Maybe being a dad wasn't something he could do better than all the other birds. Maybe he couldn't be a dad at all.

As long as the egg was still rolling around in its incubator, he ignored these prickles of self-doubt. He pretended they didn't exist. Such feelings were beneath him.

Until now. They sure weren't beneath him anymore. No, now they were on top of him. They pressed him down like bricks, making it hard to breathe, making it hard to fly! How was he supposed to be a dad when he couldn't even be *himself*?

Every flap of his once-mighty wings made Otto

doubt the universe and his place in it. What if he tumbled out of the sky and landed on the ground in a broken heap, just like Bartleby Doyle?

Holy henpeck, Bartleby Doyle!

Otto wrenched his thoughts away from his own misery and focused on the Old Man with every ounce of his strength. He scraped the outermost corners of his brain. He screwed his eyes shut, held his breath until it hurt, did some backflips, and came up with one final idea.

He would ask Pippa for help.

You might wonder why he hadn't thought of Pippa in the first place, and that's reasonable.

To begin with, Pippa was in school every weekday until three-thirty. And it was going to take a lot more than "hello" to communicate the current crisis— a whole lot more.

But now Otto saw a way Pippa could help. It was an outside chance, but he'd take it. He changed direction and flew with renewed purpose toward the workshop.

Bartleby Doyle had, at some point in the distant past, hidden a spare key to the workshop inside a fake rock. It did not "look and feel real," as advertised—not in the slightest. It looked like what it was, a lump of plastic painted an unconvincing shade of gray. Otto had stumbled upon it almost two years ago. He'd turned it over with his claw, pried open the base, seen the silver key, and appreciated the Old Man's intentions.

But it won't fool anyone, he'd thought. Especially not the way the Old Man had left it next to the door. All it lacked was a little sign inviting intruders to use it to break into the workshop. Otto spent half a day finding rocks that vaguely matched the hide-a-key and heaping them into an attractive rock garden, complete with ornamental grasses. The Old Man had forgotten all about it. So had Otto, until now.

It was to this pile of rocks Otto flew now. He extracted the fake one, opened it, and dumped out the spare key. But sticking it into a lock and turning it counterclockwise while hovering in the air was something even Otto couldn't do. For that, he would need opposable thumbs. He had never so bitterly regretted being born without them. But he had a friend with opposable thumbs, and that friend was Pippa!

He hastened, key clenched in his beak, to the

Japanese maple behind Pippa's house. Kicking aside the hamburger she'd left for him that morning, he dropped the key between the two roots.

Typically, after leaving a treasure for Pippa (and taking whatever she'd left for him), Otto would fly away. If Pippa ducked under the maple today and saw him there, why, *surely* she would understand that something was wrong. Then Otto would improvise a way to convince her to follow him to the workshop, where she could use one of her opposable thumbs to manipulate the key into the lock and open the door!

Speaking of thumbs, Pippa was at this very moment strolling home with Roberto. They were reliving the instant when Roberto had opened Julia's "present" and laughing their heads off.

They were also taking their sweet time. Ignoring all the shortcuts, they stopped at every corner for a few minutes to make sidesplitting observations to each other. Pippa was in no rush to get home. Roberto was officially the most interesting person she knew, and she had every reason to loiter and lollygag.

And so it was that Otto's plan hit its first snag.

How could he have known that today, of all days, Pippa would be late? He waited. And he waited. And he waited.

Something's off, Otto thought. *She should be home by now.*

He tapped his claw impatiently and tried not to think about the hours Old Man Bartleby had been lying on the floor. Where was Pippa? Why was she late?

Inaction felt impossible to Otto. It was agony to do nothing. He slipped out from under the maple and flew to the front of Pippa's house. He looked up and down the street, hoping to catch sight of her. There was the usual traffic, and a few people on the sidewalk, but no Pippa. Something had clearly detained her.

Otto returned to the backyard, landing on the railing of her porch. He inclined his head to the door but heard nothing to indicate she was inside. Anxious, he decided to return to the dark, cool space under the maple and wait some more.

And that was when he saw it, the grand finale to the worst day of his life.

A familiar threadbare form streaked across the

lawn. Otto watched helplessly as Marla dove under the maple tree and emerged a second later. Clenched between her ratlike teeth was the spare key.

The last thing he saw was her mangy tail as she squeezed through the hole in the back fence. Then she and the key were gone.

· 18 ·

I Love You, but You're an Alien

At that moment, if you'd asked Otto his name, or what the square root of sixteen was, or how much a five-pound bag of flour weighed, he would not have been able to answer you. His mind was a blank. He was as unthinking as a machine.

He went home. There was nothing left to do.

For the second time that day, Otto surprised his wife. This time, he didn't throw the door open. Instead, he leaned against it, almost falling over the threshold. He lurched his way to the couch, reaching the overstuffed cushions just in time.

"My goodness, what's the matter?" Lucille left the incubator and sat next to Otto.

"The Old Man's in trouble, Lu," he croaked. "And nobody cares at all."

"What do you mean, he's in trouble? What are you saying?" asked Lucille.

"I'm saying Bartleby Doyle flew into the ceiling and possibly into eternity. I'm saying he's lying on the floor of the workshop like a turnip. I'm saying . . ." Otto broke off and made a noise that sounded like a sob.

Now Lucille was truly alarmed. "I don't understand!" she cried. "I need you to start at the beginning and tell me everything."

Otto stumbled through the events of the day, stopping to clarify when Lucille had a question like "What's a Slinky?" and "Why on earth did he have rockets in his pants?" and "Are you sure they were just pretending not to understand the word 'fling'?" and "Crouton is too dumb to peck his way out of what?"

When he was done, Lucille got up and gave the incubator four or five smooth cranks. "What bothers me the most," she said, "is why you didn't tell me any of this earlier. Why didn't you mention you were going to the workshop in the mornings, Otto? Why did you wait to tell me Bartleby hurt himself? And how could you just leave him there like that?"

"I don't know, I don't know!" moaned Otto. "What was I supposed to do? I can't get inside—it's locked tighter than a drum. And the Old Man's knocked himself out a dozen times before today. I thought he just needed to sleep it off. I thought he'd be okay!"

"Otto, I'm your wife," said Lucille. "You shouldn't keep these things from me."

She collected her thoughts and weighed them with care. Otto was the love of her life and the father of her soon-to-hatch chick. He was her first thought when she woke in the morning and her last before she went to bed. He was the finest raven she had ever known.

She returned to the couch and leaned toward her husband, tugging on a few feathers at the back of his neck, straightening them out. She'd never seen him so dejected. There was something she had to tell him. It was important to choose her words wisely.

"Darling," she said, "you've been an absolute stinker."

Like every other blow Otto had endured since the early-morning theft of his peanuts, he hadn't seen this one coming. And it hurt the worst. Everything became too much.

"Gosh, Lucille. Can't a guy get a little sympathy?" he choked.

"I am sympathetic, dear. I'm just not sympathetic to *you*."

He didn't know what to say. If his own wife wasn't on his side, then nobody was. He began to cry.

As if she'd read his mind, Lucille said, "Oh, darling, I'm always on your side." She covered his back with her wing and waited for him to finish. In the entire time she'd known him, Otto had never shed a tear. She didn't want to ruin the moment.

Finally, she began to speak with great tenderness.

"Otto, I love you, but you're an alien. And by that,

I mean you alienate almost everyone we know. If you don't outright ignore them, you make them feel like you think they're stupid."

Otto blinked hard. "But most of them *are* stupid."

"No, dear, they're not. They might not be as brilliant as you are, but they do just fine. Take the 'lesser birds,' for example. When you tell them all their brains put together wouldn't fill a thimble—"

"But that's the literal truth," interrupted Otto.

"It doesn't matter if it's the literal truth. You've alienated them, and they don't like you. You've alienated your buddies, and they don't like you, either. You've alienated my brother, and now even he doesn't like you."

"Christopher doesn't like me?" Otto said.

"Sweetie, you told him he couldn't find his own butt with both wings and a map."

"That was a joke," said Otto.

"He didn't think it was funny," said Lucille. "Just like Marla didn't think it was funny when you booby-trapped the bird feeder. It was disrespectful. You alienated her."

"She's just a squirrel," muttered Otto feebly.

"And not a stupid one," Lucille said. "She gave as

good as she got. If you want that key back, you have to find her and make amends."

Otto was dumbfounded. She couldn't possibly be serious.

"That's right, amends," she repeated. "You have to admit to Marla that what you did was wrong, and you have to make it up to her."

· 19 ·

How to Make Amends
and Influence People

You have great social skills. You make amends like nobody's business. You're so good, you could do it in your sleep with both hands tied behind your back. And if there's one thing you know for certain, it's this: *saying you're sorry and making amends are not the same thing.* No, they absolutely are not.

But in case you aren't one hundred percent sure how to make amends, let's review the process. There are basically four things you need to do. Some people will tell you there are five things, or even six or seven, but if you follow these four steps, you can't go wrong.

1. Acknowledge the despicable thing you've done.
2. Listen to how it made the other person feel.
3. Validate the person's feelings by repeating what they say.
4. Apologize and ask the person how you can make it up to them.

Still don't quite understand? Wilma the mouse and Raúl the guinea pig, our pals from chapter 12, will be glad to assist you.

Imagine that Wilma has wounded Raúl's feelings by going behind his back and telling everybody in town he's a terrible dancer. In fact, Raúl is *not* a good dancer, but that is completely beside the point. Wilma isn't a judge at a dance contest. She's Raúl's friend, and she's been a lousy one. Can you spot the difference?

Word has gotten back to Raúl that Wilma has

said these hurtful things, and now their friendship is on the rocks. It's time for Wilma to make amends. Watch closely.

Wilma: "Raúl, I went behind your back and told people you're the worst dancer I've ever seen. I said you have less rhythm than a plank of wood."

Raúl: "Yes, I heard about that, Wilma, and if you don't mind me saying so, you're a . . ."

(Wilma listens attentively to how she has made Raúl feel, then repeats his words back to him.)

Wilma: "So you're telling me I'm a rotten creep and sometimes I make you feel bad so that I don't have to think about my own inadequacies?"

(Raúl nods.)

Wilma: "And you don't appreciate me telling everyone you dance like a broomstick?"

(Raúl nods.)

Wilma: "And now you feel like you can't trust me?"

(Raúl nods.)

Wilma: "I'm really sorry I said those things. How can I make it up to you?"

(Raúl thinks about this.)

Raúl: "You can go to the school dance with me."

(Wilma nods.)

Raúl: "And you can dance every song with me."

(Wilma nods.)

Raúl: "Also, we have to wear matching outfits."

(Wilma cringes and then nods.)

The thing you need to know is this: making amends isn't for the faint of heart. It's the hardest thing you might ever do. It takes real guts. But, as we shall see, it can turn you into the person (or mouse, or raven) you were always meant to be.

· 20 ·

My Name Should Be Captain Pompous

Otto circled the woods with a sack of food hanging from his beak.

"You have to follow every step, Otto," Lucille had insisted. "And don't forget step four: ask Marla what you can do for her."

"Whoa, that's seriously overdoing it," he had protested.

"Do you want the key back or not? Now hurry!"

Lucille knew vaguely where Marla lived, but didn't have her address. Her directions had gotten Otto to the general neighborhood, and it wasn't a particularly fancy one. Now he was on his own. He spotted a young jackrabbit batting around a worn-out acorn.

Otto landed softly and put down the sack. "Where's Marla?" he asked.

The jackrabbit, eyeing Otto nervously, gulped but said nothing.

"Don't play dumb bunny with me," Otto snapped. "Where is she?"

"Six oaks to your left," said the jackrabbit. "Why?"

"None of your business," said Otto, picking up the sack again.

He lifted off and veered left, counting the trees. There it was, a supremely run-down oak missing most of its bark and quite a few of its branches.

This place makes the dump look good, thought Otto.

He spotted the entrance to her house about ten feet off the ground, a dark, unwelcoming hole.

"Marla!" he cawed, settling on a barren branch not too far from her so-called door.

"Who is it?" yelled Marla.

Otto was pretty sure she knew who it was. "It's Otto P. Nudd. I have something for you."

There was a long pause. Then Marla poked her narrow face out of the darkness and regarded him sourly. She looked at the sack he carried and sniffed the air, nostrils twitching with skepticism.

"Come in," she said.

She retreated into the darkness.

Otto followed her, squeezing through the hole. In a million years, he would not have imagined himself visiting a squirrel in her home. Yet here he was, crouched in what passed for a front hallway. He looked around as soon as his eyes adjusted to the dim light. It was abysmal.

"Nice place you got here," he said.

"No it ain't," said Marla flatly.

Marla's den consisted of one room, and one room only. The walls were bare except for a shelf, which bore a rind of cheese and a scrap of muffin. A snarled mess of newspaper strips marked the location where, perhaps, Marla slept. Of chairs, tables, couches, counters, closets, or cupboards there were none. Marla was right. It was not a nice place.

A small cough drew Otto's attention to the farthest corner. There, in the shadows, were five skinny pups. They huddled together and gawped at Otto with large, frightened eyes. Between them, they shared a thin coverlet that looked very much like Marla's pelt. Otto entertained the brief idea that she had woven it from her own fur. It would explain the bald patches. . . .

"Whaddya want, Otto?" Marla asked.

Otto put the sack on the floor. It was actually a tea towel knotted around provisions Lucille had grabbed from their pantry: crackers, raisins, walnuts, and a gorgeous sunflower head filled with delicious, oily seeds. He unknotted the towel and revealed its contents. The babies in the corner began to whimper.

"You know what I want, Marla," he said.

The whimpering turned into a high-pitched keening. Marla's pups were underfed and desperately hungry. She thumped her tail against the floor until they piped down, and glared at Otto.

"You think you can waltz into my house and buy me off with a bag of chow?" she asked. "You got a lotta nerve, pal."

Otto heard her words against a rising tide of panic. He saw now that she wasn't going to make this easy. The clock was ticking—at a certain point, even if he found a way into the workshop, it would be too late for the Old Man.

But she was bluffing, right? What kind of mother would play games when her children looked like they were starving to death? He could count their ribs, for crying out loud. Marla needed food and he needed the key. Either they'd make the swap or something was wrong with her.

Marla folded her arms across her chest and glowered at Otto.

Something's wrong with her, thought Otto. *What a surprise.* Then he remembered Lucille's guidelines.

"I rigged the bird feeder with a Slinky, and that was inappropriate," he said.

"Ya think?" asked Marla.

There was a long silence. Otto moved on to the next step. "How did that make you feel?"

"How did that make me feel?" Marla asked, looking at Otto as if he'd sprouted horns.

"Yes, how did it make you feel?"

The squirrel said nothing, and Otto's hunch that his wife's four-step program might have some glitches was briefly vindicated. But only briefly.

Marla took a deep breath.

Then she let rip the foulest torrent of complaints Otto had ever heard. It was as if the dam that held back Marla's worst thoughts and feelings burst. It was cataclysmic. It was soul crushing. He listened in numb disbelief. How was it possible that any bird, let alone Otto P. Nudd, was this ignominious?

In the middle of this barrage, Otto somehow recalled Lucille's third instruction. Faltering at first, but with increasing conviction, he began to repeat Marla's words back to her. His voice rose and fell in a rhythmic refrain as he parroted her recitation of his personal defects.

"I was a complete knucklehead." "I had no business doing that." "I think I run the neighborhood, but I am very much mistaken." "I should consider the possibility that I am not God's gift to the animal kingdom." "I'm so pompous, my name should be Captain Pompous." "Who do I think I am, anyway?"

Marla went on and on. There seemed to be no bottom to her hostility. Her rancor could have filled an ocean. As it was, Otto felt like he was drowning in it. Eventually, though, she slowed down, and then stopped. Otto stopped as well. They looked at each other, exhausted.

One more thing was required, one final act of contrition. The raven stiffened his spine. Key or no key, never let it be said Otto P. Nudd left a job undone. Mastering his distaste, he proceeded to the last step.

"I'm sorry. How can I make it up to you?"

21

And as a Special Bonus

Marla was perplexed. "What'd you say?"

"How can I make it up to you?" asked Otto. His voice was mechanical now, like a robot raven. He just wanted to get this over with. In fact, as soon as the words were out of his beak, he started to back out the way he'd come in.

But Marla pounced on step four. She was all over it. "Why do you need the key?"

"That's how I can make it up to you?" asked Otto. "Tell you why I need the key?"

"It's a start," said Marla.

"I need the key to open the Old Man's workshop," Otto explained. "That is, Bartleby Doyle. He lives next door to the girl Pippa, and he—"

Marla cut him off. "I know who the Old Man is. Why're you trying to bust into his workshop?"

"It's not his workshop. It's *our* workshop," said Otto, talking fast. "And I can't use the key because I, personally, don't have opposable thumbs. So I was attempting to give it to Pippa when you—"

Marla cut him off again. "You're in a hurry. Why don'tcha save us both some time and start at the beginning?"

Otto summarized the day's terrible events, tactfully omitting the bit where Marla stole his peanuts, as well as his retaliation. She punctuated his story with grunts to indicate that she understood, and raised her eyebrows when he described Bartleby's accident.

"Oh, yeah, we're running outta time here," she said when Otto was done.

Otto felt a little surge of alarm at her use of the word "we." *That's odd,* he thought.

"We need to act fast," she continued.

Warning bells went off in Otto's brain. What was up with all the "we"? Marla was making very sloppy use of the first-person plural pronoun.

"Yes," he said cautiously, "Bartleby requires medical attention right away. He's been in there for hours."

"Three hours, to be exact," said Marla. "He's been lying there for three hours. That's an awful long time for a geezer to be unconscious."

Now the warning bells were clanging so loudly that Otto could hardly hear himself speak.

"I just need the key," he said.

"Uh-huh. And you know what I need?" Marla asked.

Otto waited.

"I need food. 'Cause I don't know if you've noticed, but my babies are hungry. Their dad got"—she leaned forward and whispered—"caught in traffic, if ya know what I mean. Things wasn't so good around here before he kicked the bucket. Now they're worse. A lot worse."

"But I brought you food," said Otto, confused.

"Yeah, thanks for that," Marla snorted. "You

brought a meal. Real nice. I appreciate it. But I need food for the duration. The long haul. I need to feed my babies till they're big enough to fend for themselves. And you know what the Old Man's got in that workshop of his? Excuse me, of yours?"

Otto knew. Of course he knew. He stared at Marla in horror.

"Peanuts," she concluded. "Bags and bags and bags of peanuts. The quantity of peanuts he's got in there could choke a horse, if you'll pardon my French. My babies could feed for a year on them peanuts."

Otto was aghast. The workshop was a hallowed place where he and Bartleby Doyle made discoveries. It was where they worked out their inventions in peace and quiet, unmolested by the mundane cares of the world. The workshop was sacred. What Marla was suggesting was unacceptable.

"It's out of the question," he said. "Those peanuts are for experimentation only. And, at Bartleby's discretion, for the occasional corvid snack."

"Well," said Marla, "there's gonna be a lot fewer 'corvid snacks' once the Old Man is outta the picture. Which, you keep running your beak, is gonna happen sooner rather than later. You asked what you could do for me? Gimme access to those peanuts. I come and go as I please for one year, and take as many peanuts as I want, no discussion. Now, what's it gonna be, Otto?"

He shook his head in anguish. How could it have come to this?

"And as a special bonus," said Marla, as if she were awarding Otto a coveted prize, "I'm gonna help you rescue the Old Man."

"That really won't be necessary," Otto said. His voice was hoarse.

"It'll be my pleasure. We're gonna need some stuff, though. Luckily, I know a guy."

22

Peak Perfection

When at last Pippa Sinclair came through her front door, she was a full forty-five minutes late. She was also giggling to herself. Her mother, who worked upstairs in her office, wasn't unduly concerned about Pippa's tardiness. She was, however, alarmed by the giggling.

"Pippa?" she called.

"Hi, Mom!" sang Pippa, giving the door a happy

slam that shook the rafters in a joyous sort of way. "I'm home!"

"You sure are," said Mrs. Sinclair. "Is everything okay?"

"More than okay," Pippa shouted up the stairs. "It's been a ludicrous day!"

She dropped her backpack. It hit the floor with a gladsome thump.

Remain calm, Mrs. Sinclair told herself as she hurried out of her office. "What do you mean, a ludicrous day?" she asked when she reached the bottom of the stairs.

"Oh, Mom, you know what 'ludicrous' means!" giggled Pippa. She threw her short arms around her mother's waist. "Today's definitely been ludicrous."

Under the guise of brushing back Pippa's hair, Mrs. Sinclair surreptitiously felt her daughter's forehead. No, she didn't have a fever. And she looked fine, if a bit peppy.

It wasn't that Pippa wasn't peppy. Of course Pippa was peppy! But giggling? Giggling was unheard-of. Pippa never giggled.

To be fair, Mrs. Sinclair wasn't much of a giggler, either. But she sure liked the way it sounded, especially coming from Pippa. *We don't laugh nearly as much as we used to,* Mrs. Sinclair brooded. *We should do more fun things together. I'll make a list. Maybe this year, she'll let me plan her birthday party. . . .*

"The party!" she gasped. She let Pippa go. There was still so much to do.

Once a year, Pippa's mother threw a party to end all parties. She invited every one of her clients (past, present, and future) and knocked herself out to make sure they had the time of their lives. It was good for business because it *was* her business: Peak Perfection Party. Mrs. Sinclair was an event coordinator. She threw parties for a living.

If this sounds fun to you, think again. It's the exact opposite of fun. Behind every great party is a person who is working her (or his) socks off. Parties involve details—more details than you can imagine. Mrs. Sinclair managed these countless details by making lists. She was nearly as famous for making lists as she was for throwing parties. Even her lists had lists. And for now, things were in pretty good shape.

"Peak perfection, peak perfection," she murmured to the sheaf of lists she clutched in her hand.

"What, Mom?" asked Pippa.

"Oh, nothing. Did you remember the party is tonight?"

Pippa fixed her mother with a look that said she hadn't forgotten the party but wasn't exactly thrilled about it. She would rather be doing almost anything else, for the reason that parties weren't her cup of tea—a fact her mother really ought to know, because if she'd told her once, she'd told her a million times. Her look said all that, and more.

"It's sure to be ludicrous," offered Mrs. Sinclair.

This seemed to sweeten the deal.

"Can I invite a friend from school?" Pippa asked.

Mrs. Sinclair hesitated. She shuffled her lists. Could she handle the additional stress of another child at her party? Probably. And it *was* nice to learn that Pippa had a friend from school, who (it was safe to assume) was neither a bird nor a senior citizen. "Does she know how to behave herself?"

Pippa thought of Roberto. Despite his trip to the

principal's office that afternoon, Roberto was generally regarded as a well-mannered individual.

"She's a he," said Pippa. "And he's a perfectly ludicrous kid."

"Oh, the best kind, then," said her mother.

· 23 ·

Marla Badgers a Badger

Back at Marla's den, the raven and the squirrel had come to the end of their negotiations.

"The key for some lousy peanuts, Otto. What's it gonna be? Yes or no?" asked Marla.

Otto chose "yes" with a stiff nod. Then he watched in amazement as Marla picked up her babies like five bundles of rags and moved them aside. She reached underneath the fetid piece of carpet upon which they'd been piled and withdrew the key. Without flourish or fanfare, she handed it to Otto.

He didn't get Marla at all. Didn't a squirrel like her need a guarantee of some sort? How could such a pathetic animal even know whom to trust? This was an unexpected display of gullibility. He disliked her, yes, but he was almost concerned.

"What's to stop me from flying away with this key and devoting the rest of my life to keeping you out of my workshop?" he asked.

Marla snorted. "You're a lot of things, Otto P. Nudd, but a liar ain't one of them. Let's go."

They left the den, with its five tiny pups who now gorged rapturously on the food Otto had brought. Marla scrambled down the oak's scabby trunk and was off like a shot.

Otto shadowed her, flying from tree to tree. He'd never been much of a follower. Letting someone else plot a path through the woods was new for him, and deeply unsettling. In fact, he hated it. But at this point, what else could he do? He followed.

"Where are we going?" he cawed after several minutes.

Marla didn't answer, but picked up the pace,

forcing Otto to watch carefully so he didn't lose her in the underbrush. She ran in a zigzag fashion, as was the habit of her species. Otto, who was accustomed to flying straight and true, hated this even more. Careening left and right was behavior unbecoming to a raven.

As they approached a particularly disreputable bank of the river that wound through Ida Valley, Marla's destination became clear.

"Badger Bend," groaned Otto. "I should have known."

"I don't like it any more than you do," snapped Marla, who heard his remark with irritation. "News flash, Otto: nobody likes this place."

"Oh, I think some folks like it just fine," countered Otto.

They drew near a mound of crumbly earth that did nothing to disguise the wide entrance to a burrow underneath. Half a dozen animals, mostly ferrets, lay about in various stages of inertia. Some were flat on their backs, legs in the air. Some were curled against each other, slack and torpid. Most were snoring. The air reeked of their yeasty exhalations.

"Ugh. Good-for-nothings," muttered Otto.

Marla ignored him and stuck her head through the opening into the earth. "Randall!" she yelled. There was no response. She shouted again and waited for a full minute. No one seemed to be home.

"I got no time for this," she muttered, dropping headlong into the darkness. "Randall!" she screeched.

Otto listened to the syllables as they ricocheted through the subterranean chambers, loud enough to wake the dead. If Randall was home, he was very committed to avoiding the squirrel.

Marla reappeared, climbing out of the burrow and brushing dirt from her pelt. "Don't say a word," she instructed Otto. "Let me do the talking."

Otto sniffed, offended. She could talk to the badger all she wanted. He'd spent his life not talking to the badger, and had gotten along quite nicely. Of course, Marla seemed to have a plan, and he didn't. The only thing to do was stand back and watch her work whatever squirrelly magic she had at her disposal. He doubted it was much.

From the depths of Badger Bend emerged the bowlegged creature known as Randall. He was low to the ground, and his back was bisected by a white stripe that ran from his nose to his bottlebrush tail.

Jug ears erupted from the sides of his head. They gave him the appearance of a friendly lummox. Neither Otto nor Marla was deceived.

"I was sleeping," grunted Randall. He blinked his bloodshot eyes in the sunlight and gave Marla a long, hard look. "Oh, it's you."

"Hello, Randall. It's been a while," said Marla.

The badger flexed his enormous paws and yawned. "How you been, Marla? I was real sorry to hear about your husband."

"Yeah," said Marla. "He's gone to a better place."

"The big tree in the sky," Randall said. His tone was unsentimental.

Marla said nothing.

"What can I do you for?" asked Randall. "Or is this a purely social call? I see you brought a friend."

This also went unacknowledged. Marla didn't so much as glance at Otto. "You owe me a favor, Randall," she said.

"Is that so?"

"You know it is."

"Who am I to argue with you, Marla?" The badger yawned again.

"I need a ball of yarn," Marla said.

"A ball of yarn," repeated Randall. His gravelly, phlegmatic voice made the request sound absurd.

"That's right," said Marla. "The biggest one you got."

"Who says I have a ball of yarn?" Randall asked. "What kind of an operation do you think I'm running here? You think we sit around all night knitting sweaters for orphans?"

"You got everything down there," insisted Marla. "You got yarn."

They stared at each other. Finally, Randall sighed and shambled back into his burrow. "This is gonna take a minute," he said as he disappeared from view.

"We got time," said Marla.

"No we don't," whispered Otto.

"Shhhh!" said Marla.

They waited in silence. After what felt like an eternity, a woolly ball of bright crimson yarn was expelled from the burrow. Almost as high as Marla's shoulder, it rolled over to where she stood, coming to a rest at her feet.

Randall did not reemerge. His voice rumbled from

the darkness. "That's a primo ball of yarn, Marla. Top quality, for old times' sake. You and I are all squared away."

"We're square," Marla agreed. "One hundred percent square. With any luck, you'll never see me again."

"Aw," growled the badger. "Now you're making me sad."

My Kingdom for a Thumb

"I see where you're going with this," said Otto. "We'll rig the yarn around your waist, and I'll lower you through the pipe into the workshop. From there, you'll somehow activate the alarm button. That's the hard part, but we'll figure it out. This just might work."

It was impressively close to the plan he'd formulated for the lesser birds. She'd come up with similar tactics. *Not too shabby,* he thought. *She's no slouch.*

"You're outta your mind if you think I'm gonna let you drop me through some pipe," Marla said. "I don't do heights, and I don't do small spaces."

"You live in a tiny hole ten feet off the ground," Otto noted.

"Not gonna happen," she said firmly. She rolled the ball of yarn to Otto. "Can you carry this to Pippa's tree?"

"Of course I can," huffed Otto.

"Good. Meet me there. We're going fishing," said Marla. And with that, she was off again, without so much as a backward glance to make sure he was following her.

Otto had a momentary pleasurable vision of tying Marla to the pipe and leaving her there. Then he sighed and, hefting the yarn in one claw and the key in his beak, flew to the Japanese maple tree. He arrived well before the squirrel did, and allowed himself this small victory.

When Marla appeared, she wasted no time in laying out her strategy. It was a simple one, and very good in the way that simple plans usually are. They would loop one end of the yarn through the key and leave it under the tree. Then they would unwind the yarn, stringing it all the way to the fence between the Sinclairs' yard and Bartleby Doyle's. Otto was to perch atop the fence with the other end of the yarn in his beak. When Pippa reached for the key, Marla would signal to Otto to tug on the yarn. Thus, the key would make its way across the lawn, and Pippa, like a fish enticed by a lure, would pursue it to the door of the workshop.

"Then what?" asked Otto.

"Then nature takes its course," said Marla. "She'll pick up the key, put it in the keyhole, and open the door."

"Humans aren't good at guessing games," cautioned Otto.

"They're not as dumb as you think," said Marla. "Nobody is. And don't forget, when I squeak, you pull."

"When you squeak, I pull," Otto said.

Clearly, he was little more than a puppet in Marla's grand scheme. But he had to admit that her plan was good. Better, even, than his had been.

They moved under the tree. In the semidarkness, Otto held the key up, and Marla struggled to thread the yarn through the hole. Then they switched and

Marla held the key steady while he tried to thread it. They fumbled as they tried to work together. It was harder than it looked.

"My kingdom for a thumb," he croaked as he aimed for the key again and again. He had never been more frustrated by his anatomical shortcoming. The yarn was fraying badly, and he could hardly see what he was doing.

"No kidding," agreed Marla. "Can you imagine how amazing life would be if squirrels had opposable thumbs? Lemme tell you something—we would rule the universe."

Get a Grip, Wilma

You know all about opposable thumbs. You probably have a pair yourself, and you're not afraid to use them. The human hand holds no mysteries for you! If there's one thing you're sure about, it's this: opposable thumbs are a huge advantage.

But in case you're not quite certain what all this talk of opposable thumbs is about, Wilma and Raúl are here to help you. Imagine that Raúl has just painted an exquisite picture of a sunset. Gripping the paintbrush in his teeth, he adds a few final streaks of orange to the canvas. Then he puts the brush down and stands back to assess his handiwork.

"Well, what do you think?" he asks Wilma, who has been watching him paint for some time.

"It's wonderful," Wilma gushes. "I wish I could give it two thumbs up. But I can't."

"Why not?" demands Raúl.

"Because I'm a mouse, Raúl. I don't have thumbs," Wilma says.

"Gosh," says Raúl. "That's a real bummer."

"Tell me about it," Wilma says. "I've always wanted thumbs. And not just any old thumbs, but opposable ones!"

"What do you mean, opposable?" asks Raúl.

"I mean the kind of thumbs Gary has," says Wilma. Their friend Gary is a chimpanzee, who has opposable thumbs not only on his hands but also on his feet! "Gary can touch the tip of his pointer finger with his thumb! He can press them *against* each other!"

Raúl is at a loss. "Why would he want to do that?"

"For the grip," explains Wilma.

"The grip?" asks Raúl.

"Yes, the grip," Wilma says. "He can pinch things. He can pull things apart. Have you ever seen Gary peel a banana? It's incredible. Think of all the things you can do with a grip like that!"

Raúl looks unconvinced. "Thumbs seem a little overrated."

"They're not! If I had opposable thumbs, it would be so much easier to pull my socks up. I could play the trumpet! I could make the okay sign! I could wear things with buttons. I could even comb my hair!" says Wilma.

"I still don't get it," says Raúl. "Why would anyone comb their hair?"

"I have no idea," says Wilma. "It just sounds fun!"

"Gee, Wilma. I never knew how much you wanted thumbs. I wish I could loan you mine," says Raúl.

"I hate to break it to you, buddy," Wilma says. "But you don't have thumbs, either."

"Yes I do," argues Raúl.

"Don't be silly," says Wilma. "If you had thumbs, you wouldn't have to hold your paintbrush in your teeth."

Raúl holds up his front paws. He looks at them and recoils in horror. "I have no thumbs!" he screams. "I'm a monster!"

Wilma rushes to her friend's side. How could she have been so insensitive? Full of remorse, she reaches up to give Raúl a reassuring hug. "You're not a monster! I'm sorry I blurted it out like that! I thought you knew!" she says.

Raúl lets Wilma feel bad for a little while. Then he laughs so hard, his jowly face hurts. "Get a grip, Wilma! Of course I knew. I'm just pulling your leg!"

Raúl is a pretty big tease, but this prank will go down in history.

"Wow," says Wilma. "Wow. You're lucky I don't have thumbs, Raúl. If I did, I'd give you a pinch you'd feel for a week."

• 26 •

Otto Resists Interrogation

Under the maple tree, Otto contemplated a horrific world in which squirrels were even more dexterous and tricky. Thank goodness their paws were thumbless—like hairy little paddles, almost. The damage they would wreak with an opposable digit boggled the mind.

At last, he hit his mark.

"Bull's-eye!" Marla said. They switched positions again, and Otto held the key in his beak while Marla looped the yarn into a knot. She tugged one way, and Otto tugged the other. The knot held.

Otto dropped the key into the place where the two roots met. He braced it with his claw while Marla unspooled the yarn across the grass. This operation was hampered by the half-dozen round tables that had been set up since the last time Otto had been there. Folding chairs surrounded each table, and three longer tables were placed at the yard's perimeter. Marla guided the yarn under the legs of the tables and chairs, maintaining as straight a line as possible from the tree to the fence that divided the Sinclair and Doyle properties.

"What's with all the furniture?" she asked as she scampered back to the maple.

"It's for an event," Otto said. "Pippa's mother is throwing a party tonight." It was the obvious conclusion.

"A party? Tonight? How do you know it's for tonight?" Marla asked.

"Because of the flowers," said Otto. There were flower arrangements on every table. "She wouldn't put flowers on the tables today if the party were tomorrow. They'd die."

"They're already dead," said Marla, who, like all animals, was mystified by the human fondness for cutting down plants and plopping them into vases filled with water. It was morbid and gross.

"All right, they'll wilt," said Otto.

"They're already wilt—"

"Trust me!" Otto interrupted. "Pippa's mother is having a party. Tonight, this yard will be full of humans."

"Okay, okay," said Marla.

"It changes nothing," said Otto. "Pippa will be along soon."

"Are you sure?" Marla asked.

"No, I am not sure. I am simply making a prediction based upon years of observation," said Otto. "Not to mention interaction." He willed himself to have patience with this infuriating squirrel, at least until they rescued the Old Man.

"Yeah . . ." Marla sat back on her haunches and monitored the yard for any activity. "About your 'interaction' with the girl. What's up with that?"

"What do you mean?" asked Otto. "Corvids and

humans have coexisted amicably for centuries. Of course, we've had our ups and downs. There was the Great War of 1838, when large numbers of crows were exterminated, but by and large—"

"I mean, how do you even know each other?" Marla asked.

Otto couldn't blame Marla for being curious (although he wanted to). Coexisting was one thing, but the raven and the girl were much closer than that. They swapped treasures and food on a daily basis. They liked each other and didn't bother to hide it. What Marla was really asking was how it all started, and *that* was personal.

"Pippa lost her father a few years ago, when I was barely a fledgling," said Otto with some reluctance. "Old Man Bartleby has helped raise her ever since. You know how much assistance human children require. In any case, you could say we've grown up together."

"Huh. I got so many questions right now," said Marla.

Oh, do you? thought Otto.

"Like, what happened to the girl's dad? And why'd the Old Man step in? Don't he got his own family?"

"Pippa's father perished in an automobile accident," Otto explained.

Marla blinked. "Just like my babies' dad!" she exclaimed.

Otto thought of the many squirrels he'd seen lying at the side of the road after an unfortunate encounter with a car. It was not an unusual fate for their kind.

"Well," he hedged, "perhaps some of the details are different. But in general, you have the right idea. It was a terrible tragedy."

Marla bobbed her head in understanding. "That poor kid," she said. "She's lucky she's got a neighbor who helps out. It's more than I got."

"Indeed," said Otto. "He saw he was needed, and he rose to the occasion. Humans will often do that, none more than Bartleby Doyle."

"What's the deal with you and the Old Man, anyway?" asked Marla. "Seems like you spend a lotta time together."

"A tale for another day," said Otto. *Or maybe never,* he said to himself.

"I think it's nice you got a pal," Marla pressed. "And interesting. Weird, but interesting. I never seen anything like it. How'd you meet?"

Otto felt he had shared enough information with Marla. She didn't need to know his life story. And time was wasting. "I'm going to take my position," he said abruptly. "Watch the door—Pippa could come out any minute." He flew to the fence.

The squirrel turned her attention to the door, which, sure enough, swung open.

But it wasn't Pippa who came out.

How could Marla and Otto have known that Pippa was pedaling her bicycle to Roberto's house to invite him to the party? It was Mrs. Sinclair herself who strode through the door, to make sure everything was in a state of peak perfection.

Both Marla, from her position under the maple, and Otto, from his position on the fence, saw Mrs. Sinclair's eagle eye fall on the bright red yarn strung under her tables and chairs.

"For heaven's sake!" said Mrs. Sinclair. "Who left that thing lying in the grass? It's a disaster waiting to happen!" She crossed the porch in a determined fashion.

"Pull, Otto, pull!" squeaked Marla.

Otto hardly needed to be told what to do. He gave

the yarn a furious tug, and the key skipped over the grass like a silver minnow.

"Pull! Pull! PULL!" Marla squealed.

He gave it another tug, and the key leapt playfully through the air, spinning and vaulting and pinging against the legs of chairs and tables. He pulled for all he was worth, like his life depended on it, like there was no tomorrow.

Mrs. Sinclair saw what was going on right away. Of course she did. She spied the glint of the key as it swam through the grass, and her eyes traveled up the yarn until they reached the raven, who clutched its vermilion end in his beak.

"Hold it right there, Otto!" she yelled. She bent over and snatched the key just as it skimmed her ankle. Then she began to wrap the yarn around her fingers, advancing toward Otto as she wound and wound and wound until she reached the fence where he perched.

Mrs. Sinclair genuinely liked Otto. If she wasn't the die-hard fan of corvids that her daughter was, she still appreciated Pippa's special friendship with the raven. She was fully prepared to indulge it for as long as it lasted. But not today.

"Not today, Otto," she said, removing the yarn from his beak and tucking everything under her arm. "And not tonight. Tonight has to be perfect—no monkey business, do you understand? I'm putting your toy in time-out."

"Hello! Hello!" cawed Otto desperately.

"Hello yourself. You can have it back tomorrow."

Marla Kicks Otto When He's Down

"Did you just faint?" asked Marla.

Otto lay where he had collapsed after watching Mrs. Sinclair carry the yarn (and key) back into the house. As a rule, Otto P. Nudd did not surrender to despair. But now he lay on his side, wings tucked around him like a black shroud.

Marla shook her head in disgust. "Get up," she said.

"Can't," he whimpered softly.

"Get up, Otto!"

Otto squeezed his eyes shut. He'd done everything he could think of to save Old Man Bartleby, and more. He'd racked his considerable brains. He'd gone to every friend and neighbor for help. He'd cut a deal with a squirrel, for gosh sakes. Now Bartleby Doyle would die and it would be his fault. How could he face Lucille after this? He'd never again be the raven she knew and loved. Nevermore.

"I said get up!" ordered Marla.

"Nevermore," moaned the raven. "Nevermore."

Marla poked him in the back with her foot.

"Lucille can raise the chick without me," said Otto, mostly to the grass into which his face was pressed. "I'll only get in the way. It's better if I just disappear."

This infuriated Marla. Now she gave him a swift kick in his tail. "You got a chick on the way?" she shouted. "Well, I got actual babies. Five of 'em, if you didn't notice. And I got nobody to help me, and it's hard, Otto. It's hard! You don't just get to 'disappear' because things didn't work out the way you wanted. Boo hoo, Otto! Boo hoo hoo hoo hoo. GET UP!"

Otto hopped to his feet just as Marla was about to give him another kick. He stared at her with what looked like real hatred. She stared back, paws on her hips, teeth bared. For a long while, neither of them spoke. Their chests heaved with fast, angry breaths. Then Marla broke the silence.

"We're gonna do it again," she said.

"Do what again?" asked Otto.

"We're gonna go fishing," said Marla. "It shoulda worked the first time. It'll work the second. I know it will."

"Insanity," said Otto.

"Whaddya mean, insanity?" Marla demanded.

"It's insane to do the same thing over and over and expect different results," explained Otto. He lacked the energy to sound condescending. It was probably what saved him from her everlasting wrath.

"Oh, right," agreed Marla. "We're gonna change it up, no doubt. For one thing, we're outta yarn."

"And outta key," said Otto.

"Yarn, key—those were just details," Marla said,

dismissing them with a wave of her paw. "We're gonna do it all over again, but we're gonna do it bigger."

"Bigger?"

"Much bigger," Marla said. "We're gonna need reinforcements."

• 28 •

String and Bling

And that was how Otto found himself racing back to the town dump for an unprecedented third time in a single day. Marla, driven by the righteousness of her cause, ran like a stallion. He shadowed her from above. They got there in a flash.

Nuddy's Buddies watched the approach of the raven and the squirrel with astonishment.

"What's going on here?" asked Crouton, half an egg roll falling out of his beak.

Jacque looked up from the greasy tangle of lo mein noodles he'd been contemplating. *"Sacré bleu,"* he said.

Fumbles and Bandit, ankle deep in sweet and sour sauce, simply stared.

Marla skidded to a stop. "Hello, fellas," she said.

Otto landed beside her and faced his friends. "Chinese," he observed.

"Yeah, it's Friday night," said Fumbles.

They always had takeout from the Golden Dragon Express on Fridays. The restaurant was generous with its garbage, and they hoarded the surplus all week long.

"Care to join us?" asked Crouton.

His tone was cautiously sarcastic. He didn't know what Marla wanted. She made him nervous. The fact that she and Otto looked somehow united in purpose was extraordinarily unnatural.

"We're not here to eat," said Marla. "Otto has something he wants to tell you."

"Wait, what?" Otto asked.

"Otto has, in the past, been rude," she elaborated.

"I have?" Otto asked.

"Very rude," Marla continued. "Now he'd like to apologize."

Crouton, Jacque, Bandit, and Fumbles moved toward each other, closing ranks. They didn't understand what direction this strange conversation was taking. Otto apologize? Their natural instincts told them something was amiss, and that their lives were probably at risk.

"Whatever you're selling, we ain't buying," said Crouton.

"Relax," said Marla, rolling her eyes. Then she glared at Otto.

So it's come to this, thought Otto. There was nothing he could do but swallow what little pride he had left. He searched his feelings and, to his great surprise, found no resistance. He *had* been rude. He'd made them feel small. He'd insulted them time and time again. He was going to apologize, and he was going to mean it.

"I . . . I . . . ," he began, and faltered. "I . . . listen, I haven't always been a good friend."

"Ya got that right," Crouton said.

The other corvids nodded in agreement but

maintained their defensive position in case they were being duped.

Otto cleared his throat and addressed them one by one.

"Crouton," he began, "your head is no bigger than it ought to be. If large heads are a sign of intelligence, then you're a genius. You come up with ideas nobody else thinks of. You've got a lot going on upstairs."

Crouton assumed a ponderous expression, tilting his massive cranium to the side.

"Jacque," Otto said, "you've been to places I couldn't even find on a map. You're an international bird of mystery, a real soldier of fortune. You give this dump a little class. I hope someday my *oeuf* will come to admire you as much as I do."

"But of course," said Jacque with a munificent chuckle.

"Bandit," Otto went on, picking up steam, "you're a handsome devil and, frankly, I should tell you that more often. The fact is I'm jealous. Who wouldn't be? You ought to be on the cover of *Birdwatch Magazine* every month. I'm serious! And, Fumbles, what you've been through"—everyone cast a glance at Fumbles's left foot, with its missing toes—"I mean, I don't even know what to say. . . ." (He really didn't know what to say.)

Fumbles grinned at the attention. He waggled his two-pronged claw bashfully. "Aw, guys, I was born this way," he said.

"Well, you make it look easy," insisted Otto. "You do a lottle with a little, as the expression goes."

The tension in the air began to melt away. Nobody had wanted to be in a fight in the first place. Jacque, Bandit, and Fumbles were mollified and ready to forgive.

Crouton alone refused to be pacified.

"It's all well and good for you to come here and sweet-talk us, but I notice you ain't apologized, technically," he observed.

"No, I haven't," Otto admitted. "Please know I am truly sorry."

"You're sorry?" Crouton asked. "Well, words is cheap. Actions is what count. The things you do."

Yes, I know what actions are, Otto nearly said, but wisely kept his beak shut. This was Crouton's moment.

Crouton had a point to make, and make it he did.

He strutted around a pile of kung pao chicken and over to a garbage heap. From this, he extracted a soiled brown-paper grocery bag, which he dragged back to the group.

"You're sorry, Otto?" he asked again. "Then get in the bag and peck your way out."

There were gasps of sympathetic outrage. "You go too far, *mon ami*," Jacque clucked. But payback had been a long time coming, and the birds were not entirely opposed to it. They waited to see what Otto would do.

He didn't hesitate.

"So be it," he said, and then he hunched, squirmed, and groveled his way into the bag. When he was fully enclosed, they folded the bag shut and stood back.

It didn't take long. Otto scratched around, orienting himself in the darkness. Then, with one thrust of his mighty beak, he punctured the bag and ripped it open. He pecked and pecked and pecked until, in short order, he stood astride a pile of shredded paper. Pieces of it stuck to his feathers like confetti. He shook them off and faced his friends with his head bowed in humility.

Then he was surrounded. A joyful mob of corvids

jostled him playfully and covered his back with their wings. They laughed and they cried and they tried to lift him onto their shoulders. When that didn't work, they jostled him some more. They shouted jokes and insulted each other gleefully. All was forgiven.

"Wrap it up!" barked Marla. "We got work to do."

The euphoria died down quickly, and Marla laid out the details of her plan, which went like this: Nuddy's Buddies were to assemble every bit of rope, cord, twine, fishing line, and ribbon they could get their claws on. Also required was anything that sparkled, including bits of broken mirrors, Christmas tree ornaments, baubles of all varieties, pull tabs from soda cans, and even jewelry. (The last demand was directed at Bandit, who sported a number of rings in addition to the pilfered diamond wedding band around his shapely ankle.) They would carry everything to Pippa's backyard without making a sound and wait there for further instructions.

It was a lot to ask. On the other hand, was it really? The corvids were on intimate terms with the dump. They owned every inch of it. They knew where the goods were hidden. They could do this.

"String and bling, guys, string and bling!" Marla said. "You got an hour. Go!"

* * *

Meanwhile, Pippa delivered her invitation to Roberto.

"What kind of party is it?" asked Roberto.

"Oh, it'll be pretty dumb," admitted Pippa. "Mostly, it's just grown-ups standing around eating food and talking about whatever."

"What kind of food?" asked Roberto.

"The really small kind," Pippa explained. "Like, if you took a normal cake, but you shrank it down so that you could fit the whole thing in your mouth all at once. Tiny hot dogs and stuff."

"Mini-muffins?" asked Roberto.

"Definitely," said Pippa.

"I'm in," said Roberto.

* * *

Marla and Otto located the lesser birds at a pool of standing water where they often gathered in the late afternoon for a quick drink before heading home.

"Yo, Smalls!" bellowed Marla. "I'm gonna make you an offer you can't refuse."

That got their attention.

"Refuse?" twittered the mustard-colored finch. "Refuse? Refuse? What is—"

"Knock it off, Elaine," snapped Marla. "I don't have time for your baloney right now."

Her name is Elaine, Otto thought, astounded. It had never occurred to him that this yellowy creature might have a name.

"Otto here needs a favor. And unless you want a personal visit from a squirrel to each and every one of your nests"—Marla's pointed gaze roved over the assembly—"I suggest you help him out. But first, he's got something he wants to say. Go ahead, Otto. Speak from your heart."

Speak from my heart? mused Otto. *To them?*

"Forgive me," he said. "I don't even know your names."

"Timothy!" chirped one.

"Celeste!" added another.

"Arlo!" the chorus continued. "Zoe!" "James!" "Milla!" "Chrysanthemum!" "Liliana!" "Victor!" "Janet!" "Daphne!" "Travon!" "Veronica!" "Ogre!"

"Did one of you just say Ogre?" Otto cut in. He couldn't help it.

A wood thrush raised his copper-colored wing and stepped forward. "I did," he chirruped. "It means 'fearless and strong'!"

He's not completely wrong, thought Otto. *That's what ogres are . . . among other things.* Otto felt no need to correct the wood thrush, which in itself was bizarre. Then he scrutinized the crowd before him, squinting and trying his best to see who they really, really were.

Bit by bit, the birds came into focus. He noticed the expressions on their faces, which were not (as he had supposed) identical. One bird was jittery, and another was inquisitive. One was modest, and another jaunty. Several were (to varying degrees) openly belligerent. One was asleep.

"No two of you are alike," he concluded.

"Yeah, they're real snowflakes," agreed Marla drily.

"Look at them!" Otto insisted. "They're brimming with individuality."

"You betcha," said Marla.

"Marla, these birds are *special.*"

Otto realized that he'd been as misguided about them as about his buddies back at the dump. They were beings who mattered, and they mattered to him.

"I'm sorry," he said simply. "I've been mean. I've been a bully. I had no right to treat you like imbeciles. Why have I called you lesser birds? You're anything but. I'm ashamed of myself. It won't happen again."

The effect of his words was electric. The birds were stupefied. Their shock was such that one of the sparrows fell into the pool and had to be fished out by her mate.

Marla patted Otto on his shoulder. It felt necessary and right. Then she gave the birds their marching orders. Each of them had half an hour to find a length of string or piece of bling and meet up in Pippa's backyard.

* * *

Pippa introduced Roberto to her mom, who ordinarily would have been thrilled to meet a friend of her daughter's same age and species.

"It's good to meet you, Roberto," said Mrs. Sinclair. "Also, I have three dozen guests who will be here in less than an hour."

"That's"—Roberto paused, calculating rapidly—"about two-thirds of a guest every minute for fifty-nine minutes."

Mrs. Sinclair's head began to throb.

"Mom," said Pippa, "I'm going to show Roberto the maple tree."

"Oh, honey, not now," implored Mrs. Sinclair. "The caterers just finished setting everything up, and it's peak perfection out there. Peak perfection. I don't want anyone in the backyard until the guests arrive."

This was no time to argue. "Fine," said Pippa. "Then I'm taking Roberto upstairs to show him my treasures." She pulled Roberto toward the staircase.

"Just a minute, young lady! Otto left something for you." Mrs. Sinclair remembered the wad of red yarn. She looked around frantically until she realized it was still tucked under her arm. She tossed it to Pippa. "There's a key in there, somewhere."

"Who's Otto?" asked Roberto.

* * *

"Otto!" shouted Marla. "Make sure the knots are tight!"

"They'll hold," Otto replied. He tested and double tested each knot.

The sun was inches above the horizon now and sinking swiftly. Mrs. Sinclair's team of workers had just left the premises. There was little time. Marla dashed about like a squirrel possessed, issuing commands faster than a drill sergeant. "Move! Move! Move!" she barked, and the birds (large and small) hastened to do as she said.

"That's five lines!" cried Crouton, tying off the final section of string.

Where there had been one line of yarn strung across the backyard, there were now five, cobbled together from string, rope, and twine. And that wasn't all. The lines shimmered. The birds had plundered their own nests for every shiny thing they could carry, and had festooned each line until it glittered in the diminishing light. They were ingenious—even artistic—and the effect was everything Marla had hoped for.

She felt the tingle of success but squelched it violently. She knew how far they had to go before they could claim victory. "Lay off, you three!" she screeched at a trio of chickadees who were quietly edging toward a pile of refreshments on a table. She couldn't let down her guard for a single, solitary second.

At last, she stationed a corvid at the end of each line. Like pied pipers, they would lure Mrs. Sinclair and her guests to the fence and direct their attention to Bartleby's workshop. Humans were bright, or at least bright enough. They would deduce that something was awry. Key or no key, they would investigate. They would find the Old Man lying on the floor. Marla was sure of it.

Otto, too, was convinced. With one line, they'd been the victims of happenstance. Now they'd quintupled their chances of success. The odds were in their favor. He glanced at Marla. *She's nothing short of a mastermind,* he thought.

Marla clapped her paws. It was showtime. "Wait for my orders," she said tersely.

"Aye, aye, Captain," said Fumbles.

She did not object to the way that sounded.

29

An Item of Beauty Is a Joy Forever

"This is so cool," whispered Roberto.

Pippa lifted the top tray out of the tackle box, revealing a second tray and a third. She and Roberto were sitting crisscross-applesauce on the rug next to her bed. It was the first time she had ever shown someone all the things Otto had given to her.

"You mean he brings you this stuff in exchange for food?" whispered Roberto.

Pippa shook her head. "Not really," she said. "Otto gets his own food. It's just his way of telling me he's thinking about me."

"And vice versa?"

"Yep. Otto likes chicken nuggets the most," Pippa said. "But he also likes Tater Tots."

"Seriously? Because I *love* Tater Tots," whispered Roberto.

"Well, they are delicious," said Pippa.

"But how do you know his name is Otto?"

"Mr. Doyle told me," said Pippa. "He lives next door. He's an inventor. He and Otto work together."

"You are kidding me," whispered Roberto, awe-struck. His voice was so low that Pippa had to lean forward to hear it. Their foreheads almost touched. Slowly, Pippa took each treasure out of its compartment and passed it to Roberto, who examined it with the reverence of a museum curator before putting it back.

"My favorite item is the Eiffel Tower," said Pippa, handing a key chain to Roberto. A miniature golden replica of the French landmark dangled from its links. So beautiful was this souvenir that, among all the treasures in the box, it was the only one Pippa called an "item." The key chain exhibited no tawdry signs of wear. Uniquely, it had no rust. None of its links was broken. It was no mere "thing."

"Wow," whispered Roberto. "It's incredible." He suspended it from the tip of his finger, letting it swing back and forth like a pendulum. "You should put the key on it."

"What key?" asked Pippa. Now she was whispering, too.

"The key Otto left for you. The key inside the yarn," answered Roberto.

Pippa was confused for a second, but then she remembered. She stood up and retrieved the ball of red yarn she'd tossed onto her desk when they had come upstairs. Roberto stood up as well. He held on to the end of the yarn, and Pippa unwound the ball until she reached the key in the very middle. She untied it and, fiddling a little, managed to attach it to the ring on the key chain.

"You keep it," she said, handing the key chain to Roberto.

"But Otto gave it to you," said Roberto. His

objection could barely be heard above the ringing of the doorbell as the first guests arrived.

"Otto won't mind," said Pippa. "He definitely won't mind at all."

She spoke in such a low murmur that you almost had to be a lip-reader to understand her words. But Roberto grasped their meaning perfectly. He attached the key chain to his belt loop.

Pippa wondered how it had taken her so long to realize what an awesome kid Roberto was. He was one of her oldest friends. Why was she only seeing it now? They'd done so many things together—a ton of things! They'd probably gone to the same nursery school (although that was ancient history and Pippa couldn't remember). They'd moved up through every grade at Ida Valley Elementary together. He was in all of her school pictures. They'd been in school choirs and gone on field trips together. But until today, she'd never noticed how much she liked him. She couldn't wait to introduce Roberto to Otto. She knew Otto would like him, too.

The two of them sat back down on the rug and continued to sort through her treasures. They admired the exceptional ones, and also admired each other. They practically didn't even need words, or at least not loud ones. They were happy to be quiet together. The amber glow of Pippa's bedroom lamp cast a peaceful radiance over everything, lasting a long, long time, until it was shattered, all at once, by Mrs. Sinclair's scream from downstairs.

30

Raccoons Are Terrible People

This is where we must rewind the story a little to understand the bloodcurdling scream that sent Pippa and Roberto racing downstairs.

Mrs. Sinclair did not indulge in drama, ever. A true professional, she remained serene under pressure. In fact, she was a legend in the business. The parties she planned were her only concession to theatrics, and she executed them like a four-star general.

Tonight, each table in the backyard groaned under the weight of fall flowers. Interspersed between wild cascades of autumnal leaves were sweet daisies, bundles of lavender, clusters of snapdragons, and ravishing blush roses. Every florist in the valley had jockeyed to provide the most extravagant blossoms.

Among these horticultural profusions, woodland figurines were arranged impishly. Bunny rabbits played hide-and-seek with hedgehogs, and fawns frolicked with foxes. Every animal was fashioned from blown glass and polished to a limpid sheen.

What's more, the punch bowls, cups, platters, and dessert stands were made of Bavarian cut crystal. Taken together, they glinted like a constellation of jewels.

Antique chandeliers with untold numbers of crystal prisms hung from the long branches of an oak tree in a corner of the yard. They seemed suspended in midair, as if by some enchantment.

All was designed to catch and refract the beams of light emitted by hundreds—no, thousands—of electrical globes strung back and forth above the tables.

Mrs. Sinclair conceived a dazzling fairyland, one that would spring to life as soon as she hit the power switch. This harmonized fantastically with Marla's "string and bling" installation. The woman and the squirrel were visionary geniuses.

Marla made sure the birds were in their places as Mrs. Sinclair led the first guests to the door to the back porch and beyond. Pausing in her immaculate kitchen, Mrs. Sinclair flipped the switch that lit the yard. The scene erupted in a blaze of glory. It was staggering in its otherworldly beauty. Everyone gasped with delight.

And then Mrs. Sinclair (and Marla) screamed.

Unbeknownst to either of them, raccoons from one end of Ida Valley to the other had been watching the party preparations with intense fascination. On the other side of the back fence, they had sidled up to each crack and knothole. There they stood, a horde of them, pressing their nasty faces to the splintered wood, spying, quivering with excitement.

Someone had tipped them off. It might have been Randall, whose weekly kickback from the raccoons was sizable. Probably not, though—the badger truly did have a soft spot in his heart for Marla, and for all widows. Anyway, it doesn't matter. They were all there, staking out Pippa's backyard.

Raccoons manage their public image brilliantly. They are often portrayed as soft, cuddly black-and-white pranksters. "Cute" is a word often applied to raccoons. What a farce. In reality, they are some of the vilest creatures you will ever meet. The havoc they can wreak on a chicken coop in less than thirty seconds is barbaric.

Generally, raccoons prefer to operate under the cover of darkness. Mrs. Sinclair had thrown a number of parties in her backyard without a single raccoon showing its loathsome face.

Tonight was different, though. Tonight there was a colossal amount of bling. Sure, there was also every kind of fragrant, appetizing delicacy piled high on tables. Raccoons will certainly sneak food if they can get away with it. But it wasn't the food—*it was the bling!* Raccoons are incapable of resisting anything shiny.

Marla's long lines of suggestively glimmering yarn called out to them. They yearned to get their repulsive little hands on all that sparkly stuff. It made them squirm with desire. And Mrs. Sinclair's resplendent displays on the tables and in the trees sent them over the top. In the luminous minutes between day and night, they leered at the twinkling yard. If only they could get in there and take what they so desperately wanted with every odious fiber of their beings.

They began to dig, quietly at first, but with growing urgency. There were no humans to discourage them, and soon they had excavated a trench beneath the fence that was almost large enough to squeeze through. Another minute or two and they'd be in.

Then Mrs. Sinclair flipped the switch, and the raccoons went out of their minds. When the light from a thousand bulbs hit the profusion of glass and crystal in that yard, bouncing from surface to surface, it was like being inside a diamond. It was the bling event of a lifetime. A team of bloodhounds could have been patrolling the yard, and it would not have stopped the raccoons. They were utterly out of control.

They poured under the fence in torrents, blinded by their longing to fondle and possess all the lustrous things. Platoons of raccoons shoved their way into the yard. The grass seethed with them.

Pippa's mother did not fully comprehend what she was seeing, and neither, at first, did Marla. But Otto knew at once what was at stake. Ravens (and crows and jays and jackdaws) sleep at night, and raccoons sleep during the day. Rarely do their paths cross. But when they encounter each other, watch out. It is never pretty.

"Attack!" he screamed to his fellow corvids, calling them to battle. "The enemy is at hand! Take no prisoners!"

Otto had never seen war and (as has been said) despised combat. But the mantle of commander-in-chief fell naturally on his shoulders. He led the charge at the first wave of raccoons, beating them about their heads with his wings and forcing them to fall back. The other corvids followed his lead, and it looked as if the crisis might be averted. Unfortunately, they were sorely outnumbered.

"Otto!" shrieked Marla from under the maple. "They're going after our lines! They'll ruin everything!"

"I can see that!" Otto called back. "Organize the

birds! They can create confusion—it's what they're good at!" He returned to the fray and disappeared from Marla's view.

Marla looked around the yard frantically. The glare from the party lights was blinding. She blinked hard, trying to clear her vision. Where were the finches, the nuthatches, the wood thrushes, and the chickadees? Then she spotted a large battalion of them clustered around the bird feeder. They seemed to be taking instruction from, of all birds, the very house sparrow who was their occasional tormentor.

". . . gotta dive-bomb 'em!" she heard him say. "Wings in, beak out, feet back! Watch me!"

Bravely, he launched himself from the bird feeder and rose high into the air. Whirling around, he aimed straight for the closest raccoon, and fell from the sky like a missile. His aim was true, and he struck his target hard. *Thunk!* Raccoon and sparrow lay on the ground, dazed and temporarily incapacitated. The bird managed to fly away before the enraged raccoon took a swipe at him, but it was close.

His narrow escape didn't discourage the rest of the birds from trying it. Like a hive of hornets, they dive-bombed the raccoons for all they were worth, and kept at it for a long time. They suffered almost every injury you can think of. Many of them had to be carried to the sidelines by friends when they were too battered to continue, but their heroism bought Marla some time to do what she did next.

Namely, she left the field of battle and went recruiting.

31

This Is Better Than TV

The humans watched avidly as the skirmish un-folded. Mrs. Sinclair was flanked by her guests on one side and Pippa and Roberto on the other. After screaming, Mrs. Sinclair had clapped her hand over her mouth and stood there, horrified. What could she do but watch helplessly as her career flushed itself down the toilet? She certainly wasn't going outside. That way lay madness.

Pippa and Roberto pressed their faces against the window, hardly daring to breathe. "He's out there— I know he is," said Pippa.

"Who is?" asked Roberto.

"Otto," said Pippa. "He has to be."

But it was hard to see who was doing what. To be blunt, it's difficult to tell ravens and crows apart when they're moving fast. Feathers and fur were flying everywhere, and the screeching and yowling of the raccoons was enough to raise the dead.

The doorbell rang, and when nobody answered it, another raft of guests let themselves in. They included the mayor of Ida Valley and her husband. The newcomers followed the noise into the kitchen and joined the assemblage watching the clash in the backyard. Half the guests had begun to root loudly for the birds, and the other half for the beasts.

"My gosh, this is better than TV," said Mayor Kravetz, removing her coat and elbowing Mr. Kravetz aside for a better view.

It was when Marla returned with Christopher and the junior brigade of ravens that things reached a fevered pitch.

Christopher, as you recall, was Otto's brother-in-law. He and his gang of friends nursed military ambitions, and played war games in their spare time, which is to say all day long. Older ravens, saddled with the responsibilities that came with adulthood, found them quite aggravating. Otto could hardly tolerate them. That is, until now.

"Brother!" he shouted. Not brother-in-law, but brother. "Brother, help us save the string!"

He motioned to the glistening lengths of string, which no longer ran in neat parallels across the grass. The raccoons were dragging them to the trench under the back fence, where they might abscond with them into the woods. The corvids were doing everything in their power to prevent this.

"Bravo," murmured Mayor Kravetz. "I've never seen anything so well orchestrated in my entire life."

Mrs. Sinclair, who had been on the brink of dialing Animal Control, slipped her phone back into her pocket.

"I don't know how you do it, Adele. You're some sort of crazy magician!" The mayor turned back to the window. "This is a triumph!"

"Is it?" asked Mrs. Sinclair.

"Where on earth did you get those birds?" asked

the mayor. The birds, their brains muddled from so much dive-bombing, were now simply doing figure eights in the air. "Outstanding. I want them for the next Fourth of July flag raising."

There was a murmur of accord among the guests, and then a roar of excitement. They had spied a squirrel, long and lean, racing down one of the refreshment tables. Brandishing a serving spoon between its teeth, it hurdled a pile of cucumber sandwiches in a single bound and then, grappling the tasseled end of the table runner, swung itself into the middle of the fight.

* * *

Marla hit the ground running. The battle had distilled itself into five fearsome games of tug-of-war between the corvids, on one end of each string, and the raccoons, on the other. Otto, Crouton, Jacque, Fumbles, and Bandit anchored a line each, and were helped by dozens of junior corvids. Marla darted into enemy territory, rapping raccoons sharply on their knuckles with her spoon when she could, and causing them to lose their grip. It was dangerous work.

"One, two, three, pull!" shouted Otto at regular intervals. And for a while, the sides seemed evenly matched. But then the corvids started losing ground. Only Crouton's team held its position, but that was because his line had become hopelessly entangled with the legs of a chair, which started moving back and forth with each heave and ho.

It's over, thought Otto.

He called to Christopher to take his place as anchor, and flew up to the fence between Pippa's and Bartleby's houses. Like a general taking stock of a battle, Otto surveyed the scene below. The birds, large and small, were giving everything they had to the fight. Many had dropped with exhaustion. Some had lost blood. They were heroes, and he loved them for it.

And that magnificent squirrel! He watched as Marla zigzagged between the lines, striking blows where she could with the massive spoon. He was prouder of her at that moment than he could possibly say. Her plan had been solid. She'd been a champ. They'd tried their hardest. But they were losing. It was indeed over. The Old Man was done for.

"Hello!" he wailed. "Hello! Hello!"

32

Pippa Almost Loses Her Head

"That's him," whispered Roberto. "That's Otto. It's gotta be."

He pointed to the lone corvid on the fence, his majestic silhouette stark against the rising moon.

"Yeah, it's definitely Otto," said Pippa. Something was off—she could tell from the tragic angle of his beak. Without another word, she grabbed Roberto's hand and pulled him out the front door. She didn't think anyone would notice their hasty exit, and no one did.

Together, they ran toward the fence where Otto was perched, nursing his grief. They stopped well before they could be seen by the party inside Pippa's kitchen. "Otto, hello!" she cried. "What's wrong?"

Otto flinched, startled to hear his own name. He had almost given up hope that Pippa would come to his aid. But she was here now, with a short, bespectacled boy in tow.

"Hello!" he said. *I needed you! Where have you been?*

"Hello!" said Pippa. *I'm sorry. You seem really upset.*

"Hello!" he replied. *You can't imagine. There's no time to explain.*

He took a step in her direction, then ran all the way along the top of the fence, toward the street. He stopped and looked back at the children.

"I think he wants us to follow him," said Roberto.

"Of course he does," said Pippa.

She and Roberto ran after Otto, who jumped off the end of the fence and waited for them on the ground. The three of them did an about-face and started around the other side of the fence—that is, Bartleby Doyle's side.

They ran past Bartleby's house. The lights were out, but this didn't strike Pippa as strange. Didn't all old people go to bed as soon as the sun went down? They crossed his backyard, lit brightly by the lights on the Sinclairs' side of the fence. Otto led them behind the workshop and then flew up to the window ledge. He gave the glass three or four urgent pecks.

"I think he wants us to look inside," said Roberto.

"Of course he does," said Pippa. "But it's too high."

"You'll have to climb up on my shoulders," said Roberto gallantly.

"No, you have to climb up on mine," sighed Pippa. It just made sense. Small as she was, Roberto was smaller.

"Of course I do," said Roberto.

Pippa crouched low. Roberto obliged her by taking his shoes off. He swung his left leg over her left shoulder and his right leg over her right shoulder. She raised herself slowly, her legs wobbling. Roberto reached as high as he could, grasping the ledge with his fingertips for balance. Then he stood up.

"Ow! Ow!" she yelled. "You're stepping on my hair!"

"Sorry!" Roberto said.

"You're twisting my head off," Pippa complained. "I'm being decapitated by your smelly socks."

"Everyone's socks are smelly," Roberto said calmly. His eyes barely cleared the windowsill. They were level with Otto's ankles, actually. Roberto looked up at the raven, who was staring into the dark workshop.

"What do you see?" asked Pippa.

"Not a thing," said Roberto. "I'm not tall enough." He slid off her back, trying not to pull her hair.

Otto began to hop up and down with anxiety. He cawed with anguish.

"Otto," said Pippa, rubbing her neck, "we don't know what you want."

"Hello! Hello!" said Otto, flying back to the ground. His voice took on a pleading tone. He gestured to the workshop with his beak.

"I think he wants us to go inside," said Pippa.

"Of course he does," said Roberto. "There's a situation in there."

They raced each other to the door, where they took turns jiggling the doorknob.

"It's locked," said Roberto. "You have to tell your mom. She'll know what to do."

"She won't leave the party," countered Pippa. "Not now. Her head is probably exploding this very minute."

"Then we have to call the police or something!" insisted Roberto.

"And tell them what? That Otto thinks there's a situation inside Mr. Doyle's workshop?" asked Pippa. The police didn't know Otto. They didn't know he was the smartest bird in the world.

Pippa and Roberto turned to Otto for more guidance.

"Caw!" he screamed. "Caw! Caw!"

Why weren't these kids doing anything? Why weren't they kicking the door down? They were fifteen times bigger than he was. What was stopping them? He kicked his leg forward and backward, then to the side, karate-style.

"I think he's having a seizure," said Roberto.

Otto thought maybe he *would* have a seizure.

But then a miracle happened. In the moonlight, he saw the gleam of the Eiffel Tower hanging from Roberto's belt loop. He knew that item well—he'd been extremely pleased with himself when he'd left it under the maple for Pippa. More to the point, Otto recognized the key. In a flash of brilliance that happens perhaps once in a lifetime, he understood what to do.

"Key! Key!" croaked Otto. The new word felt strange in his throat, as if he'd accidentally swallowed a cough drop. He tried to get it just right. "Key! Key!"

"Is he saying 'caw' or 'key'?" asked Roberto.

"'Key,'" said Pippa. "He's definitely saying 'key.'"

It was as if a thunderbolt struck them at the same time. "The key!" they screamed in unison.

Roberto yanked the Eiffel Tower off his belt loop and thrust the key into the lock. He turned it sharply and heard a click.

Pippa pushed the door open, but Otto charged past them. He whooshed into the workshop and flung himself against the emergency button. He hit it so fiercely, he almost dislocated his wing.

From there, things happened in a blur. Pippa turned on the light and saw Bartleby Doyle. He was still on the floor, cold and pale. In an instant, she and Roberto were kneeling by his side. Roberto tried to feel for a pulse. It seemed like the thing to do under the circumstances. He couldn't tell if he felt anything or not. He gave up and ran back to Pippa's house for help.

The paramedics, responding to the emergency button, got there just as Mrs. Sinclair was dialing 911. They were followed by the police and fire department. Once inside the workshop, they found a young girl crouching next to an old man, holding his hand and trying hard not to cry. Bartleby Doyle was carried on a stretcher through a crowd of people who had streamed out of the Sinclairs' house at the sound of the sirens. He was loaded into an ambulance.

"Is he okay?" Mrs. Sinclair asked. "I'm his neighbor."

"He's breathing," said a paramedic. "He's had a bad fall, but he's a tough old bird. We just need to warm him up. He'll be home before you know it."

Do you promise? Pippa wanted to ask. Her eyes filled with tears, and then she really did start crying.

"Well, we're going with you," said Mrs. Sinclair, putting her arms around her daughter.

"Sorry, ma'am. You'll have to follow us to the hospital," said the paramedic.

* * *

After the ambulance took Bartleby Doyle away, there were no more big surprises. Well, perhaps there were one or two, but they didn't happen until later.

Mrs. Sinclair and Pippa drove Roberto home. Then they went to the hospital to sit with Bartleby Doyle until he regained consciousness. And he *was* a tough old bird. He woke up with several ideas for improvements he and Otto could make to their flying pants.

The animals left the battlefield. In the end, the birds let the raccoons steal some of the bling, and then they chased them off the property. Everyone felt like they had been on the winning side.

The humans went back inside, and Mayor Kravetz commandeered the party. Everyone had a fabulous time, and it was generally regarded as the event of the decade. Mrs. Sinclair's business prospects multiplied like rabbits.

Nobody noticed a worried squirrel patrolling the edges of the yard, looking for her friend. Neither did they notice the raven who had walked into a cage behind some filing cabinets in the workshop and was now crooning softly to himself.

• 33 •

Mechanical Advantage Strikes Again

"What are you doing in there?" asked Marla.

The workshop was empty except for the raven and the squirrel. She stood on the table in the middle of the room.

"Oh, I'm just taking a little rest," said Otto.

"Inside a cage?" asked Marla.

"Yes," said Otto. "I was practically raised inside this cage. It's very homey."

Actually, he hated the cage. But it had been a good place to remain inconspicuous while the paramedics worked on the Old Man.

"I see they left the door wide-open," he observed. "That was thoughtful. We'll have to think of a way for you to get in when Bartleby and I aren't here. You know, for the peanuts."

"For the peanuts," Marla repeated.

As her eyes became adjusted to the darkness, she caught sight of the bags of peanuts against the opposite wall. The sheer bounty of food made her go weak in the knees.

"How's everything next door?" asked Otto.

"It worked itself out, believe it or not," said Marla. "Fights can't go on forever, you know."

"Fights can't go on forever," Otto agreed.

"You shoulda been there," Marla went on. "I always thought your buddies were a bunch of useless sacks, but now that they've finally done something worthwhile, they're walking around with their feathers puffed out to here." She stretched her paws in front of her chest.

This made Otto laugh. "We'll see how long it lasts," he said. He left the cage to join Marla on the table.

"The humans are really partying it up," said Marla. "They better leave some scraps."

Otto realized something. "You never stop thinking about food, do you?"

"Can't afford to," said Marla.

They sat there for a while, listening to the sounds of the festivities. Apparently, it took a lot more than the arrival of an ambulance to keep humans from having a good time. Otto had to respect their dedication.

"What do you mean, you was raised in that cage?" Marla asked suddenly.

"I mean I was raised in that cage. I fell out of my nest when I was barely hatched. I don't know where my parents were—off hunting, maybe. My leg was broken, and so was my wing." Otto paused. It was not a memory he visited often. He'd been so cold, and so afraid. Where had his parents gone? It was the terrible mystery of his life.

Marla waited patiently.

"Bartleby Doyle was walking through the woods, and he found me like that," Otto went on. "He took me to a doctor and then made a roost for me inside a shoebox. When I outgrew the shoebox, he put me in the cage. I don't think he knew what else to do."

It had never occurred to Marla that Otto's origins could have been so harrowing. "I have a real hard time picturing that," she said.

"It's true," said Otto. "He named me and fed me and talked to me about the experiments he was working on. Taught me all sorts of things. But he kept me in the cage, and I loathed it. A true raven will not be shackled, you know. A true raven will not be kept."

"So they say," said Marla. "How'd you get outta there?"

Otto's face brightened. "I used science! How much do you know about mechanical advantage?"

"Not a whole heckuva lot," said Marla.

"Let me explain it to you this way," said Otto. "I slept on one of Bartleby's shirts. One night, I ripped a sleeve off and soaked it in my water bowl. Did you know cotton fabric is stronger when it's wet? Well, it is. I tied the sleeve around a couple of the bars and stuck a ballpoint pen in the knot, like a lever. Then I turned the pen around and around. The sleeve got tighter and tighter, until it pulled the bars apart. I stepped right through them. When the Old Man came in the next morning, I was sitting on top of my cage. He was stupefied! After that, I came and went as I pleased."

Marla pictured his escape. She was overcome with wonder. This bird was a marvel.

"Why, you sly son of a gun," she said.

Otto accepted the praise with a nod and a shrug. He doubted his jailbreak had ever been equaled, let alone surpassed. "It was the pen, you see. The pen gave me mechanical advantage. When it comes to mechanical advantage, you can't have too much of a good thing. It helps you perform feats of strength that, on your own, would be unimaginable. It's like . . . it's like . . ."

"It's like the friend you never knew you had?" prompted Marla.

"Yes," said Otto. "Just like that."

· 34 ·

A Bird for the Ages

"Otto! Otto! Otto!"

Christopher, still riding high from the night's campaign, flapped through the door.

"Otto! The egg is hatching! The egg is hatching!" he yelled. "And guess what! Potato is twins! Ha ha! Twins! That's why he was so gigantic! Twins!"

Christopher did a couple of laps around the workshop and then left as quickly as he'd come in.

Otto sat paralyzed with dismay as his brother-in-law's news sank in. Twins? The word seemed to echo off the walls of the workshop. Twins was twice as many as one. Lucille was waiting for him with two little chicks. They needed him right now, on the double. Yet he couldn't seem to make his wings move. He felt numb.

Marla cleared her throat.

"Congratulations, Otto," she said. "You know what? I'm just gonna wrap up a few of these peanuts and hustle home. The babies start crying for their breakfast at the crack of stupid, no matter what."

"You mean the crack of dawn?" asked Otto faintly.

"Nope," chuckled Marla. Now she was on the floor, dumping peanuts into a cocktail napkin she'd borrowed from the party. "I mean the crack of stupid, as you're about to discover. Kids never let you sleep. It's, like, their sacred duty or something."

She glanced up at the raven. It was dark in the workshop, but she could make out his expression. He looked panic-stricken. Marla stopped what she was doing.

"Hey, you did great today," she said. "You saved your friend's life."

"I couldn't have done it without you," said Otto.

"Ha! My plan was a flop!" Marla said this cheerfully, as if failure was nothing new to her, which it wasn't.

"I disagree. Your plan was ingenious," said Otto. He was determined to be fair, if nothing else.

Then Marla did something extraordinary, at least for her. She climbed back onto the table and put a paw on either side of Otto's beak. She shook his head back and forth.

"Otto, it's hard to take care of people. But guess what! You already take care of people. You take care of our neighborhood. You're going to be a terrific dad."

"You really think so?" asked Otto.

"I do," said Marla.

He wasn't sure. He didn't remember anything about his father. He had only known Bartleby Doyle, the man who had carried him home in the palm of his hand and done his best to give him a life. Was *that* what being a dad was? And not to be ungrateful, but the Old Man had put him in a cage, then raised him to be an inventor. Otto wanted to raise his chicks to be true ravens, unshackled and free. How was that done, exactly? He had no idea. None whatsoever.

On the other hand, could a squirrel like Marla be mistaken? Otto didn't think so. It's not often that someone comes along who is both a decent friend and a brilliant military strategist. Marla was both these things, and more besides. She was brave and scrappy and dreadfully honest.

Otto decided to believe Marla. If she said he'd be a terrific dad, then a terrific dad he would be. Mistakes would be made. Blunders would occur. He might even have to ask for help once in a while. How lucky for him that he had Lucille, Marla, Pippa, and (he hoped) Bartleby Doyle.

He had, in fact, an entire legion of friends.

His thoughts were interrupted by the flutter of another pair of wings. These belonged to the mustard-colored finch. She landed on the corner of the table and smirked.

"Whaddya want, Elaine?" asked Marla.

"Lucille sent me," warbled the finch. "You must fling yourself home, Otto. Fling home! Fling! Fffffling!"

Then she turned around and, with a sassy shake of her tail feathers, flew back out.

"That is one wicked little bird," fumed the squirrel. "Someday she's really gonna get it."

"Oh, I don't know, Marla," said Otto in a voice that sounded practically fatherly. "She's starting to grow on me." Then, impulsively, he asked, "Care to meet my chicks? Of course, you're needed at home. Don't feel obliged."

Marla hesitated. She'd been gone for a long time, and she did need to check on her own babies. It was late, she was exhausted, and she'd never been the guest of a raven before. It wasn't really done. But all the same, there were more reasons to say yes than to say no.

"I'll come for a few minutes," she said. "Race you there!"

She was out the door while the words still hung in the air.

Otto won, but not by much. There was hardly space for him to squeeze into his own nest, teeming as it was with well-wishers. Even his buddies from the dump were there to see the chicks.

Otto pushed past everyone to the bed where Lucille was lying.

"Lu," he said. "Lu, twins!"

Lucille laughed and raised her wings to show him the tiny chick nestled under each one. "Meet Ambrose and Bettina, dear. They're perfect."

The chicks were unspeakably ugly, as all baby corvids are, with the ghastly blue eyes of newly hatched ravens. Otto gazed at them, his heart melting with adoration. He motioned to Marla, hidden in the back of the crowd, to come forward and admire his brood.

Birds shuffled this way and that, opening a corridor for this uncommon guest. If there was anything stranger than twins, it was the appearance of a squirrel at a time like this.

"Very nice, Otto," said Marla. "They look just like you."

Otto beamed with pride.

"Do they have middle names?" she asked.

"Oh, right," he said. "Middle names are my job. Well, if Lucille agrees, the boy will go by Ambrose B. Nudd. That's B for Bartleby. It's a family name."

He looked to his wife for confirmation, and she gave him a tender nod.

"As for the girl," he continued, "the name by which she'll be known in Ida Valley is Bettina P. Nudd."

"No, Otto, no," gasped Crouton. "Good gosh, what're you thinking? You can't saddle her with a name like Perpendicular. She'll never forgive you!"

"*I'll* never forgive you," said Bandit.

"Me neither," echoed Fumbles.

Jacque just shook his head, appalled.

Otto laughed, and it was the laugh of a raven who knew he was surrounded by friends who liked him as much as he liked them. The woods themselves were full of friends. In fact, not counting the odd raccoon, Ida Valley was overrunning with the friends of Otto P. Nudd.

"Oh, you birds," he said. "You birds and you squirrel! You're all wonderful, did you know that? P is for Pippa! Not that there's anything wrong with Perpendicular."

And then he thanked them for their kind attentions to his family, ushered them out of his nest, got into the soft bed with Lucille and the chicks, and fell fast asleep.

A Note About Corvids

Are you familiar with the story from Aesop's fables about a crow and a pitcher of water? The crow was thirsty, but the water in the pitcher was too low for him to reach. Or maybe it was just that his beak wasn't long enough. Either way, the crow found a tidy solution. He dropped pebbles into the pitcher and raised the level of the water. Then he took a nice, long drink.

Would it surprise you to learn that crows are every bit as clever in real life as the one in the story? Scientists have tested them by re-creating the conditions in Aesop's fable. (In at least one case, they floated a tasty worm on top of the water, just out of reach of the bird's beak.) Sure enough, crows dropped stones into the container until the water was high enough for them to drink (or get the worm)!

If crows are terrific problem-solvers, ravens are even better. They know how to make and use tools. They are so good at recognizing people that researchers who work with them occasionally resort to wearing masks! If you annoy a raven or crow, they'll remember your face for a long time. Likewise, if you become their friend, they won't soon forget you.

It can be hard to tell crows and ravens apart unless you're an expert. I've been paying attention to them for years, and I still mix them up. They're so similar, you might wonder if they can interbreed. In other words, can they make little "cravens"? The answer is they *can,* but they almost never *do.*

Corvids have family and friends and enemies. They fight and play games. They feel happiness and sorrow and paranoia. They have good days and bad ones! They use gestures, won't team up with birds who annoy them, and like to show off. It's not a stretch for me to imagine a raven like Otto P. Nudd, bird for the ages. Perhaps you'll meet a crow (or a squirrel, or a badger, or a human) in this book who reminds you of someone you know!

Acknowledgments

Thanks must be given here to animal lovers everywhere. I did not grow up with a particular interest in animals, although I had a pet monkey who liked to sneak into my bedroom and ransack it. By and large, I was interested in people and their preoccupations. But with age has come a fascination with the greater animal kingdom. I am, like Bartleby Doyle and Pippa Sinclair, especially beguiled by corvids—their intelligence, habits, histories, and family matters. (And ravens do take the cake.) I thank the zoologists, amateur and professional, who are generous with their knowledge of these phenomenal birds. I owe a particular debt to Bernd Heinrich, author of *Mind of the Raven*. In a more general way, I am grateful for my subscription to *National Geographic*!

Gabi Mann (of Seattle) came to my attention in

2015, when I read about her incredible relationship with the crows in her backyard. I thought, "This is the kernel of a story if ever there was one." Miss Mann was the inspiration for young Pippa, whose friendship with Otto carried her through a really rough patch.

Once again, I thank Steven Chudney, who is the very model of a hardworking, book-loving, super-smart agent. Phoebe Yeh, editor extraordinaire, has been determined, wise, and kind in her quest to help me write the best book of which I am capable. I am indebted to Elizabeth Stranahan and her gift for detail that drives a book toward completion, and who is so gracious in the process.

My children (William, Camille, and Isabelle) are my fundamentals. They're my first and last audience and have become valuable sounding boards. Dave, thanks for making space for me to write. Nobody sees the long game better than you, or prizes a good book more.

I remember Richard C. Hughes, my high school physics teacher, with love and gratitude. He was one of the finest teachers I have ever had, and he implanted ideas about science, invention, and humanity that I hope are reflected in *Otto P. Nudd*. Teachers can have a lifelong impact. I still think about Mr. Hughes standing in front of the class, quietly and with good humor demanding the best from us. Mechanical advantage!

About the Author

Emily Butler's debut novel, *Freya & Zoose,* received a starred review and first purchase recommendation from *School Library Journal. Otto P. Nudd* was inspired by the many times Emily and her dad walked to their subway stop behind a venerable neighbor who paused every few feet to take a peanut out of his pocket and leave it, mysteriously, on the rail of a fence. Emily is the eldest of seven children and grew up hiding behind the sofa so that she could read in peace and quiet. (It was never quiet.) She finished high school in Brazil, worked on a kibbutz in Israel, practiced law in New York City, catered weddings in London—and was never without a book in her backpack or briefcase. Emily lives with her husband in an old house that is stuffed to the gills with three lovely but disobedient children, and every sort of book.

Take off in your next Emily Butler adventure!

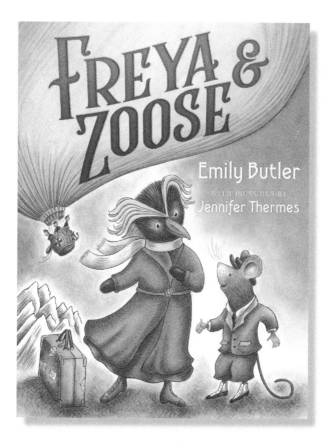